CW01671737

TIM

A growing up tale for grown-ups who remember . . .

L. L. ROSE

LITTLE QUEST PRESS

CHAPTER ONE

Atlas had flown back to Valencia because his mother was to be celebrated by the Romance Languages Department. He couldn't afford to be away from his studies at McGill, but no way was he going to miss this. He'd have to delay meeting with his supervisors; and after all, research on *music in linguistics* wasn't going anywhere.

"They've decorated the hall in red and white for Canada," his mother said. Her face was lit like a Christmas tree. "And I've been told the playlist features a fine selection of reggae music in honour of my Jamaican heritage. Your dad would have loved that."

"Yes, he would," agreed Atlas. It was wonderful to have his mom all to himself for lunch, but he was preoccupied.

"Félix doesn't look well," he said.

"No," agreed his mother. "They say he's clear, but I'm not so sure. He's still losing weight."

"Is he going for more tests?"

"Yes. He says the weight loss is normal and he's fine, but I insisted."

"Good." Atlas felt a twinge of fear. He didn't want to imagine the prospect of his mother losing a husband a second time—and of he and Peter losing their second father.

"Maybe that's all there is," said his mother.

"Yes, maybe."

A little later, he headed to the city centre to pick up Peter, who was coming on the train from Bern. "Don't rush back," his mother said. "Go for coffee. Have a good catch-up first."

"Yeah, that'll be good," said Atlas. He hadn't seen his younger brother in a long time.

He got off the metro at Colón and walked towards Plaça de Ajuntament. It was a bit early to go to the station.

He put on his headphones and turned on some reggae music. He wasn't the reggae fanatic he knew his dad would have wanted—not even much of a fan—but when his mother had mentioned reggae, it made him want to listen to some of his dad's old tapes. They'd long ago been converted to MP3s. The sound quality wasn't great, but they were live recordings, and all the noise and interference made it easy for him to imagine his dad and his band, sharing their art, eking out their living in smoky bars in Calgary and Edmonton and, later, Toronto. Atlas shook his head, a little sadly, thinking of how his dad had so appropriated his mother's culture; how, when he was very small, he had wanted to be just like his dad.

Atlas wandered, taking in the grand buildings and avenues. He remembered how awestruck he'd been, years ago when they first came. He'd hardly been outside Calgary at that age. Europe was a revelation, and he had decided on the spot to become an architect when he grew up. Of course, he changed his mind when he realized the mathematics involved, but he was still enchanted by it all.

Enchanted.

He never would have guessed. He had so dreaded coming to Spain.

With these thoughts weaving with the reggae in his head, he turned off Plaça de Ajuntament and walked down Carrer de la Sang and—

No! It couldn't be!

He quickened his pace, speeding around the dawdling tourists who so clogged the city centre these days, and then ran outright, until he was standing directly in front of it. When had this happened?

Tim Hortons, the sign said in that familiar script, in giant red letters. He opened the door.

Inside, it was quiet and air conditioned with small brown tables and simple brown chairs. Row upon row of iced doughnuts gleamed in the glass cases at the front, and the fragrance of brewing drip coffee filled the air, all exactly as he remembered it.

He texted Peter. "I won't be at the station," he said. "Come to the corner of Carrer de la Sang and Sant Vincent Màrtir and we'll have coffee." It wasn't far for Peter to haul his suitcase—only a few blocks—and when he got there, he'd understand why.

Atlas sat down in a slippery, hard chair, with the firmness that had so comforted him, and he was swept back to before they'd moved here. He was eleven and he so desperately wanted to grow up—to be a man and shoulder the responsibilities he thought he should take. He smiled and was sad, all in the same moment, feeling for that boy—that boy who used to be him. Now, with his mother and Félix's health to worry about, not to mention finances, exams, and so many other things, he thought he'd rather have stayed a boy for longer.

How innocent he'd been! Well, that was his mother's intention all along, putting him and Peter into that independent school. No computers allowed, no TV. Yes, at age eleven, he was very, very sheltered. Thank goodness Peter had always been an omnivorous reader and a good researcher, or there were some things they might never had found out. He shook his head; but smiling a little.

He heard someone order in English and looked up. A wandering Canadian tourist, no doubt, lost and making a beeline to something familiar. "A double-double," the man said. Yes, it was still just the same.

CHAPTER TWO

It scared him, that weird feeling he had when he looked at her. Atlas knew he should be listening to Mr. Wick, but he couldn't drag his eyes forward. To the side, he could see her right arm resting on her desk, so narrow, with blonde fluff glowing in the sunlight from the south windows. He shifted. Her freckled face was scrunched up as she took notes, her messy hair falling down her back. She started to turn, and he looked away.

"What?" she hissed.

He met those piercing eyes, so pale they almost weren't blue.

"Nothing," he said. "I was just . . ."

"Just what?"

"I—I was trying decide if your arm's skinnier or mine."

"What?"

"I meant . . . I mean . . ."

Harper gave him a sideways look and turned away, strawberry-blonde cascading over her shoulder, as if to block him out. The strange sensation plummeted, dropped into his boots, and he looked down. That was the wrong thing to say. What *were* you supposed to say to girls? Why did she make him feel so weird anyway? He didn't know and he didn't know who he could ask. Campbell would laugh at him for sure, and probably spread rumours that he was in love with Harper. The thought of it made his cheeks burn. He sneaked a peek at Campbell, two rows over, long ago separated from him because of their inability to listen when seated together. Campbell, as usual, was tapping out a drum beat with his pencils—but very quietly.

"All right, that's enough lecturing," he heard Mr. Wick say. "We'll have a quiz at the end of the week—"

What? A quiz? What had Mr. Wick been talking about?

"—but let's put these language arts skills into practice now with something fun. A lot of you are in hockey and some of your dads help ref or practice with you, and they teach you the skills they've learned." He turned to write on the board, "So I want you to write a little essay on *Why My Dad is My Hero*."

Harper's skinny arm flew into the air and her hair fell back in waves.

"Mr. Wick!"

"Yes, Harper?"

"Some of our moms help, too, like my mom, she coaches my team. Can we write about *Why My Mom is My Hero*?"

"Yeah!" said Kelsey, at the desk behind Harper.

"Harper, I've just said that the assignment is *Why My Dad is My Hero*. I think that's quite clear. It's not *Why My Mom is My Hero*."

"But why? Girls play hockey and my mom—"

"In any case, it would be 'heroine' not 'hero' if it was about your mom—"

"Heroin!" crowed a tall boy at the back. "That's drugs!"

"Thank you, Isaac," said Mr. Wick, with a quelling frown. "As I'm sure you know, *heroine* is the female form of the word *hero*." Isaac sniggered loudly.

"Why isn't hero the male form of heroine?" said Parjeet, with his serious round face. He was always asking questions like this. Harper talked over him.

"Why can't we write about our heroine?" said Harper.

"Because this assignment is about your hero—your *father*, Harper."

Harper started to speak. Atlas loved how feisty she was; that she played hockey and was never scared of the teachers. She looked ready to give Mr. Wick a telling-off. But Mr. Wick clapped his hands and said loudly, "Now! The topic is not up for discussion. Let's get going and if you concentrate, you can get it done during class. If not, it'll be homework."

Harper's mouth squeezed into a frown, but she turned her scribbler to a fresh page and picked up her pencil. Atlas looked down at his blank page. He hadn't written any notes on whatever Mr. Wick had been lecturing on, and now he was supposed to fill his notebook with some stupid story about his dad. He punched his arm into the air.

"What is it, Atlas?" said Mr. Wick.

"Why can't we write about another hero?" he said. "Not our father?"

"That's enough! I'm not going to repeat myself. The topic is clear, and it's written right in front of you. Start with your name and the date at the top, as usual. It's on the board there: *Tuesday, February 3, 2004*. Now get going!" and Mr. Wick walked to the back of the room, leaned against the wall, and folded his arms. The class recognized this as his patrolling mode. From there, he could see what everyone was doing and hand out detention slips to miscreants—which he often did. Everyone got down to business.

Atlas glared at his blank page and poked it with his pencil. Not sharp enough. He went over to the pencil sharpener, taking his time to crank it slowly until he got a perfect, lethal point. He could feel Mr. Wick's eyes on him. He dawdled back to his desk. The blank page stared at him and he poked it several times again with his pencil and now he got jagged holes. Satisfying. Satisfying and also useless, because if he didn't get writing, he'd have homework and that would cut into his hockey time. So, he wrote:

My dad is not my hero. He was a pothead and all he ever did was go to bars and taverns and play his stupid drums, until he left for Toronto and never came back, and then he got himself killed walking drunk on the road at night. He was a loser and he's not my hero. My hero is Tim Horton.

He looked at what he'd written. Then he tore the page out and crumpled it up and sat with his arms folded. After a couple of minutes, he heard Mr. Wick come up from behind.

"What's the trouble here?" he said. "Writer's block?"

"No, I'm done," said Atlas.

"You haven't taken enough time to put in a decent effort, Atlas. Let's get going."

"I'm done!" he said, louder than he'd intended. "Here!" and he threw the crumpled page at Mr. Wick.

CHAPTER THREE

That was why he was sitting outside the principal's office at the end of school, listening to Mr. Wick's and Ms. Martin's voices rise and fall. Mr. Wick sounded aggrieved and Ms. Martin sounded vexed. Snippets floated through the door:

"... when you know his father is dead ..."

"... not really the point ..."

"... not an appropriate assignment! ... absentee fathers ..."

"... he threw ... !"

"... don't ... again ..."

The door banged open and Mr. Wick came out looking angry.

"He'll need a warning slip," he said to the secretary; and to Atlas, "In the future, I expect you to treat both your assignments and your teacher with more respect. If you ever hand in a crumpled page again, it'll be an automatic zero."

Atlas nodded.

Ms. Crampon hoisted herself awkwardly from her desk. She had a bad leg—frozen-knee syndrome, she said—and she didn't enjoy getting up and down, but she never complained.

"Wait a minute, dear," she said to Atlas, and walked to Ms. Martin's office, careening a little. Atlas heard her say, "He didn't tell me what I'm supposed to put on the warning slip."

Ms. Martin spoke quietly, but he could hear her. She gave a long sigh: "Just put 'classwork incomplete' and leave it at that. *Every* year, somebody thinks it's a smart idea to have kids write about their parents and there's always some child who's lost theirs or is estranged, or . . . Why, Irene, *why*?"

"I'll put 'classwork incomplete,' then," said Ms. Crampon, and she retraced her unsteady steps, groaned down into her chair, and wrote out the note.

"Here you go, Atlas."

"Thanks." He whisked it from her hand and rushed out of the office, where he nearly bumped into Campbell, who had been waiting.

"You got detention?" said Campbell, doing his usual head-duck-eye-blink. Campbell could look a bit twitchy if you didn't know him, but Atlas knew him. He wasn't twitching, he was being serious. "Wick looked steamed when he came out."

"No," said Atlas, "I just got a warning slip from Ms. Crampon."

Jimmy Zimlinski happened to walk past at that moment. He was the oldest student in the school, having been held back twice, and was by far the biggest and meanest. He sniggered, "You got your cramp on, Mizz Tampon?"

"Shut up," said Atlas to Jimmy's back—but not so that Jimmy could hear him. Then to Campbell, "He *always* says that. What's it supposed to even mean?"

"He's an idiot," said Campbell.

"Yeah, I mean, what is a tampon, anyway? It—" he stopped at the look on Campbell's face. "I mean, I know what it *is*, but it's just lame," he ended lamely. He didn't really know. He knew it had something to do with women, and maybe even girls, and he had seen pictures of tampons on TV. But what women did with them was a mystery. Campbell had older brothers, so he knew things. Of course he knew, he always did, and he often teased Atlas about his innocence. Well, what was he supposed to do? He only had his mom and Peter at home, and even though Peter read constantly and everyone said he was a genius and he knew a *lot*, he was only six. Atlas couldn't ask *him*.

Atlas jammed his hands into fists and jammed his fists into his pockets and hurried forward. "We're gonna be late for practice," he said.

Atlas was grateful he hadn't been given detention. And Mr. Wick hadn't said he should do the assignment for homework, so he wasn't going to. He was never, never writing an essay on how his father was his hero.

At hockey practice, he played ferociously. In his mind's eye, he played low in the corners like Tim Horton had, keeping the puck between his feet until he could burst out from behind the net ready to make a play. Campbell was a lot bigger and heavier than Atlas, and he tried to imagine himself at that size. Coach scolded him for trying to play offense, but in the end he said, "Boys, Atlas has just given us a prime example of hard-hitting play. That's the way to do it. You don't need to make stupid choices that land you in the penalty box. Just make good, clean hits. That's the way to channel any aggression you might be feeling."

This last was the only indication that Atlas' tough play was related to the language arts assignment—which, of course, Coach knew; for Coach was Mr. Wick. But he insisted on keeping his two roles completely separate. When he was Coach, he wore jeans and a leather bomber jacket rather than the usual button-down shirt with argyle vest. As Coach, he was tough, but talked to them in a friendly way, like he was their friend. Mr. Wick, on the other hand, was fussy and strict. And woe betide the boy who accidentally called Mr. Wick "Coach" or vice-versa. He said this separation was important for the different kinds of respect each role demanded and for the boys' own mental well-being. Whatever this might mean. Adults were always saying weird stuff, but Mr. Wick more than most. The boys just shrugged and carried on, and on this particular day, Atlas felt relieved that Coach seemed not to care that Atlas had earlier flung a wadded-up page in Mr. Wick's face.

After practice, the boys piled into the bus and, as he always did, Coach said to Mr. Esposito, "Let's make a little stop on the way." And then turning to the boys, "How about . . . ?"

"Tim Hortons!" shouted Atlas. Mr. Esposito groaned. Gavin Eccles said, "Not Tim's again! McD's!"

Some of the boys started to chant "Timmy's! Timmy's!" and Gavin Eccles and Luis Lamenca cried, "McD's!"

"I'm never taking you to McDonald's," said Mr. Esposito, "so forget it. Do you know the environmental—"

Coach cut in. "Tim Hortons it is."

"Oh, for the love of coffee," said Mr. Esposito, "can we not just once go to Bean Planet?"

"TimMY'S, TimMY'S!"

"Come on, Mr. Esposito," said Coach clapping him on the shoulder, "lighten up. You can get Timbits. Let's go."

They fooled around on the bus in a way that Mr. Wick would never have let them and made more noise than marauding chimpanzees on the way in. Coach ordered small hot chocolates all around. Atlas cupped his hands around his cup, feeling its warmth. He breathed in the smell of coffee and the slippery seats and felt the hard surface of the smooth, brown table beneath his elbows. On the wall was a framed photo of Tim Horton standing at centre ice in a face-off pose. Here, at Tim Hortons, Atlas didn't have to explain himself to anyone, and it was exactly the same every time. Here, he felt at home.

CHAPTER FOUR

Atlas heard: "Pass me the *pimentón, por favor*."

"*Voilà*," his mother said.

Atlas groaned. Not Félix, *again*. Félix had been dating his mom for a while, and now he was a fixture of the family. Today, Atlas wished it was just his mom and Peter and him. He dropped his hockey bag and peered around the corner into the kitchen. His mother and Félix were squeezed into the tiny space, cooking together and mixing up their languages, as usual; and they looked happy. Atlas turned away.

"Is that you, Atlas?" called his mother. "How was practice?"

"Fine," said Atlas and stumped towards his room.

"What? No kiss for your mother?" called Félix. Atlas' mother said, "Don't be silly," and then there was laughing, and Atlas closed the door to his room and shut out their sounds. He slumped onto his bed and looked over at Peter's, where his brother sat reading next to a pile of library books. He had an open notebook in his lap, where he frequently added something with a coloured pencil. That was Peter: either reading or drawing, or reading *and* drawing, with his glasses sliding down his stubby nose. He said drawing helped him remember what he read and that it was easier than trying to write things with his underdeveloped six-year-old fine motor skills. Peter's other main activity was following Atlas around and trying to be part of whatever he was doing. Atlas didn't know why, but he knew Peter looked up to him a lot; and though he knew the trailing along would irk someone like Campbell to the point of wrath, he couldn't get angry with Peter. Instead, he felt a great weight of responsibility. He thought he should protect his younger brother and teach him things; only he didn't know what or how.

Atlas reached under his own bed for a comic book. Then he remembered he'd left his hockey gear sitting in the bag. His mom was pretty easygoing about most things, but that wasn't one of them. Sloughing off this annoying task was very much not worth the shouts of being a smelly ape that would follow. He hauled himself back off the bed and went to the balcony with his boots. It was snowing lightly. He rammed his feet into his Sorels and stepped into the dark and quiet, leaving the door open just a crack so he could feel the warmth and smell the cooking smells from inside. It was peaceful. He grabbed the basket of frozen pegs and started to hang up his gear. Their apartment didn't have a mud room like Campbell's house, so he had to hang his gear on the balcony. His mom couldn't stand the smell indoors.

Did he really smell like an ape? He lifted his shoulder pads to his nose. They just smelled like playing hockey.

He went back indoors, mulling this over, and headed to the bathroom. Girls often said that boys stank. He wondered what boys were *supposed* to smell like. He looked in the mirror, shrugged. Atlas in the mirror shrugged back. He took off his shirt and lifted his arm to smell in his armpit. It smelled a bit sweaty, sure, but did it stink? "How'm I supposed to know?"

He looked up and a face was looking at him: a man's face, with smiley eyes and an eyebrow with sparse outcroppings that stretched across the bridge of his nose to meet in the middle, a straight nose, a crooked smile, and a jutting chin.

"There sure is a lot to know, isn't there, Atlas?" the face said.

Atlas opened his mouth to scream, but instead a yelp got strangled in his throat, and he bolted out of the bathroom and careened into his bedroom, slamming the door behind him. Peter looked up, blinked.

"Where's your shirt?" he said.

"There was—Peter—!"

"What?"

"Wait here."

He dashed back to the bathroom, then stopped at the door. How could someone just appear in the mirror and speak to him? He peeked into the bathroom. It was still and silent. He stepped inside, averting his eyes, his heart pounding ferociously. Slowly he lifted his eyes.

"Hi, Atlas. Where'dya go?"

He shouted and slammed the door shut behind him. "What—why—what!"

"What am I doing here?"

"Y-yes!"

"I'm just here to help you out, buddy."

"Wh-wh—"

Atlas reached out a trembling arm and touched the mirror. The face was still there. It smiled at him.

Atlas stuttered, "B-b—you can't—you're—"

"Dead?"

"Yeah!"

"Yes, I am."

"Then you're a ghost?"

"Just your buddy in tough times, Atlas."

"N-no!" and Atlas ran back to his room, once again banging the door behind him. He stood panting, shirtless, with his back and his hands pressed against the door as if to keep out the enemy. Peter put down his book.

"What's going on?"

"I—I—Peter, come with me!"

He ran back to the bathroom and Peter followed. Atlas slammed to door shut. In the distance, he heard Félix call, “Boys, please—all that noise!”

“Look, look in the mirror!” said Atlas. Peter was small for his age and he had to strain on his tippy toes, so Atlas grabbed him around the waist and hoisted him up. “What do you see?”

“Us,” said Peter.

“Nothing else?”

“Nope.”

Atlas dropped Peter with a plunk.

“Not—you didn’t see a face?”

“Mine and yours.”

“No, not your face, another face.”

“Like what?”

“Peter, I could see—I saw—I saw *Tim Horton* in the mirror! And he talked to me!”

CHAPTER FIVE

Peter wasn't like other people. He didn't express surprise or disbelief or try to talk Atlas out of what he'd seen; he just looked curious and started asking questions. Atlas' answers clipped off most of them.

"—Just now!"

"—Yeah, he talked to me! He said he was here to help me."

"—I don't know!"

"—No, I never saw him before! Or anyone!"

"—It was real! He spoke to me! He called me buddy . . ."

"Why can't *I* see him?" said Peter, finally getting out a full sentence without being cut off.

Atlas shrugged. "I don't know. I was just smelling in my armpit, trying to figure out if I'm stinky like Mom says, and there he was. I'm not crazy!" He followed this up with: "I'm going crazy, aren't I?"

They stood in silence for a moment, and then Peter said, "Do you think you're going through puberty and it's making your brain—?"

"Puberty? What's that?"

"It's when your body starts to change so that you turn into an adult. You start to make hormones—"

"What's that?"

"—and you grow hair in your armpits—"

Atlas lifted his arm. Underneath was smooth.

"—and facial hair—"

He definitely didn't have any of that.

"—and pubic hair—"

"What's that?"

"It's hair that grows round your privates."

"Like—around—what?" Atlas looked at Peter with alarm.

"Yes, all men have it."

"Does it—how long does it get? Do you have to cut it?"

Peter frowned. "I don't know. I never thought about that, and the book didn't say."

"Is that why some men walk that way? Do they have to—like tie it up with an elastic or something when it gets too long?" Atlas was appalled. "Then how do you—doesn't it make a horrible mess when you go to the bathroom? How do you keep it clean? Is that why men smell so bad?"

"I don't know!" said Peter, now looking worried as well. "I'll have to find a book . . ."

"Well, I'm definitely not going through *pube*—whatever!"

"Puberty."

"I'm not!" said Atlas, and he stalked back to their room and sat on his bed, forgetting that he didn't have a shirt on and forgetting to read comics and feeling confused and afraid. Peter came back in a few minutes later.

"Mom says to tell you supper's ready."

❖

He was preoccupied all the next day. Why didn't he have someone he could talk to? Why did he have to rely on his baby brother? Peter read so much that he knew a lot of things, but it wasn't natural. Older brothers were supposed to tell *younger* brothers things, and here he was, more ignorant than a six-year-old. All he could think about was his crotch, and it was starting to itch. And he was afraid he would start scratching right in front of everyone. By lunch time, he couldn't stand it.

"I have to talk to you," he said to Campbell.

"What?"

"In private, though."

"Okay," said Campbell, turning to a quiet corner.

"No, outside," said Atlas, and he headed to his locker and got his boots.

"Why can't we just talk here?" said Campbell behind him, but Atlas carried on down the hallway, and he heard Campbell grumble and then start to pull on his boots.

Atlas stood with his back against the frozen brick wall, looking towards the chain-link fence at the perimeter of the schoolyard. Campbell came up next to him.

"What's going on?" Campbell followed Atlas' gaze to the fence.

"I need to know something," said Atlas.

"What?"

"I don't have anyone to ask or else—well, you've got older brothers."

"What?"

"Don't laugh, but—do you know about public hair?"

"Public?—oh!" Campbell laughed. "You mean *pubic* hair!"

"I said, don't laugh!"

"Yeah, but it's funny."

"Stop! I need to know!"

"Well, it grows around—"

"I *know* where it grows. But how long does it get? How do you keep it from getting smelly? Do you have to cut it? Do you have to tie it up? Does it make a big ball, or—"

"What?" and a huge guffaw burst out of Campbell. "Pratless!" he crowed, using the name he saved for special, humiliating occasions.

Atlas punched him. "Stop! Stop it!"

But Campbell only howled louder.

"Stop! It's not funny!"

"Oh, yes it is!" said Campbell, holding his sides.

"Stop!" shouted Atlas, hitting Campbell in a non-winter-gear-protected part of his body—i.e., his face.

"Ow!"

"Well, stop then! It's not funny. It's okay for you, you have Ethan and Everett and your dad to ask. I've only got Mom and Peter."

"Oh, man, that's too funny!" said Campbell, and then seeing the look on Atlas' face, quickly added, "But it's nothing weird or scary, right? It's just a little bit of hair. You don't have to do anything special."

"No special—like, special shampoo or something?" This set off Campbell howling again. Atlas picked up a handful of snow, threw it in Campbell's face, and stomped back into the school.

"Sorry, bro!" he heard Campbell call; but still laughing. He felt upset through the rest of the day.

So, this time, when Tim Horton appeared to him in the mirror in the bathroom, Atlas wasn't terrified or worried about losing his mind; he was eager and impatient.

"What do I call you?" he blurted. "Do I call you Mr. Horton?"

"Well, hello, buddy," said Tim Horton, grinning that small, upturned grin of his, set within that long, strong chin. "You can call me Tim, like just about everybody. My close friends call me Timmy, but I think Tim'll do."

"Okay—Tim. Can I ask you a question?"

"That's what I'm here for."

"How am I supposed to find out about growing up? I don't have a dad or big brothers, and I asked Campbell an important question today—a really important question—and he *laughed* at me. Do you know who Campbell is?" Atlas could feel frustrated tears trying to get up there in his eyes, and he blinked.

"Yeah, I do," said Tim. "That stings to have a friend laugh at you."

"Yeah . . ."

"He didn't mean to be mean, though. He just found it funny."

"I know. But it's not funny! Who am I supposed to ask about stuff? Peter finds out everything from books, but books never tell you the important stuff, and anyway, I'm his big brother. I'm supposed to help *him*."

"That's the truth," said Tim.

"I mean, I got the answer to my question, but what if I have another question like that tomorrow?"

"You're bound to have."

"Can I just ask *you* next time? Will you tell me the honest truth without laughing?"

Tim was quiet and looked thoughtful for a moment. "You know, I never had a boy of my own. I had four daughters."

"Oh, yeah! I know—Tracy, Kelly, Jeri-Lyn, and Kim."

"That's right."

"Did you feel bad that you didn't have a son?" said Atlas.

"No. And here's an important thing, Atlas: don't regret things. Be grateful for what you have."

"Oh—okay, I—" and Tim Horton's face faded away. "Wait! You didn't tell—can I ask you?"

Atlas stood there waiting, but Tim Horton didn't reappear, and eventually Atlas trailed off to his room, wondering what Tim had wanted him to understand.

CHAPTER SIX

He'd discussed it with Peter, and Peter, as usual, sat reading and drawing in his notebook and listening. But he didn't have much to say. So, now Atlas lay in bed thinking: *Be thankful for what I've got. Well, what've I got?*

He did the inventory. Mom and Peter. His dad was dead, and his grandparents were both dead, and his dad had been an only child. So, there was no one left from the McAdams family. The Raphael family, on the other hand? His mom's clan was too big to keep track of, but in all of the sprawl, there were only two uncles: old Uncle Fitzroy, who had gone back to Jamaica and whom Atlas had never met; and Uncle Liron, who was right here in Calgary; but . . . Atlas rolled Uncle Liron around in his mind. He *was* a grown-up. At least—he was in university. But he didn't seem very grown up. And he didn't feel like the kind of person Atlas could go to for advice. Grown ups were sensible and serious, and that wasn't Uncle Liron at all.

Who else? He thought about neighbours and his teachers and all his hockey coaches, and even Campbell's dad. He didn't trust any of them enough to ask them for advice. Not for the kind of help he needed. Félix popped into his head, but he dismissed that thought immediately. *Definitely* not.

Well, he'd ask Tim about it next time.

Atlas rolled over and went to sleep.

❖

The very next day, he needed help. On Thursdays, gym was first period. They did circuit training, which about half the girls and at least the same number of boys hated. Atlas knew why: it was plain hard work. But Atlas had read about what a hard worker Tim Horton was, and how he spent a lot of time doing chin-ups and push-ups to develop his upper body strength. Apparently, that was something hockey players didn't do back in Tim Horton's day. Atlas thought proudly about how Tim Horton had been ahead of his time, and now, all hockey players worked to build up not only speed and endurance, but upper body strength, too. Atlas went straight to the chin-up bar and started pulling.

It was torment; and it frustrated him that he could only do a few in a row. Mr. Diallo said that was average for an eleven-year-old, but he didn't want to be average. He wanted to be incontrovertibly a gentleman and a hard worker. That's what they'd said about Tim Horton. He dropped to the ground, shook out his arms, went again.

"Get off the bar!" said Isaac, pushing him from behind. Atlas did a lap around the gym, then came back. After a few rounds of this, Mr. Diallo called, "Raphael, you're not following the circuit! Get on with it." Atlas got on with it . . . for a couple of minutes, and then came back to the chin-up bar. After a few more episodes, Mr. Diallo told him off and sent him to the corner to do crunches. "Your arms aren't going to magically pop muscles in once day, Atlas. This isn't Toon Town." Everyone laughed and Atlas' face burned, but he didn't mind too much. Crunches were good for core strength, and that was important, too. He'd seen photos of Tim Horton shirtless, and his abs were like rippled cement. By the end of gym, Atlas was sweating and exhausted, and he felt he'd done well.

By next period, though, he was despondent. He grinned at Harper as he took his seat across the aisle from her, but she wrinkled her nose. She turned her head away and pulled a bunch of her long hair partway over her nose. Atlas was alarmed. Did he smell bad? He put his nose down towards his armpit surreptitiously and sniffed. Oh, man! He stank! He spent the rest of the morning feeling as if he were under a spotlight with a big stamp across his forehead saying ROTTEN. He tried to lean as far away from Harper as he could, and Mr. Wick snapped at him to sit up straight. Atlas wanted to crawl in a hole.

At lunch, he could hardly eat. He opened his lunch box, and a windup toy leapt out and lurched across the table, spinning and making a large noise disproportionate to its size as it frantically unwound itself. Heads turned in curiosity. Peter sometimes pranked his lunchbox, and this would normally have made him laugh, but today he didn't want to be the centre of attention. He grabbed the toy and shoved it into his pocket, then turned and cornered Campbell. "How much money have you got on you? Can I borrow some? I'll pay you back tomorrow."

Campbell blinked at him, ducked his head; then he dug in his pockets. "I don't just carry around money," he said, but when he pulled out his hand, he was holding a toonie. "Sweet! I didn't know I had this."

"Thanks!" said Atlas, swiping it up and pelting out of the room.

"But, I didn't—what's it even for?" called Campbell.

Atlas knew he should tell his best friend what was going on, but this was too embarrassing. He dashed on his coat and boots and ran out the side door, through the broken space in the chain-link fence at the back, down Orr Street and onto McDonald. He wasn't supposed to be off school property, but this was an emergency. Two minutes later, he skidded into the drugstore at the corner of Unger Avenue.

What was it that people used to stop themselves from stinking? Oh, yeah, deodorant. He'd seen a hundred commercials about it but had never once given it any thought. He went up and down the aisles, reading the signs. Beauty, baby, vitamins . . . Where would it be? Personal grooming? He stopped at long shelves jammed with tubes and bottles, and he didn't know where to start. In front of him were a lot of pink and white things, so that wasn't right. He moved along. Blue and green? Wait! There was black!

He ran to other end of the row. He could tell from the names and pictures that these were the men's products, but which was the right one? There was anti-perspirant essence, body spray, deodorant spray, deodorant stick, roll-on anti-perspirant, roll-on advanced, absorbent powder, extra dry—he didn't know what any of these things were! He forced himself to breathe and slow down so he could examine the labels. A clerk walked by and he thought, with horror, that she was going to ask if she could help. He walked away quickly. Then he circled back from the other direction. After much deliberation, he settled on Axhead Anti: Men's Supertough Deodorant. He grabbed the bottle. But turning it upside-down, he read, *$4.15*. What? That was more than twice as much as he had!

He went up and down the aisle, frantically searching the prices. Finally, he came to baskets at the end labelled *Travel Size*. There lay a tiny tube in neon fuchsia priced *$1.50*. It was the only one he could afford. He took it to the counter and felt his face go red as the clerk rang him through.

Atlas rushed back to school, into the bathroom, into a cubicle, and locked the door. He opened the tube. He'd seen on commercials how people sprayed or rolled these things on. This one was a rolling kind. He lifted each arm and rolled. He could still smell a sweaty tang, so he rolled more and then started to sneeze. The smell was strong—and flowery! He put his arms down. Maybe the sickly-sweet smell wouldn't come out too much if he didn't lift up his arms?

Back in class, he kept his arms clamped tight to his sides, but he could still smell the perfume. It was Social Studies, one of Atlas' favourite classes, and they were studying black history in Alberta as part of Black History Month—a topic which interested Atlas because of his Jamaican heritage. When Ms. Balfour asked about Caribbean influences in the provinces, Gavin Eccles said, "Pirates of the Caribbean!" which she ignored.

"There's lots!" burst out Atlas. "Jerk chicken and roti, and Calypso—"

"Hand, please, Atlas," said Ms. Balfour. Atlas kept his arms clamped tight to his sides. He put up his left hand, but it didn't rise above his head. No way was he putting it higher and letting out the foul, flowery perfume. Ms. Balfour arched her eyebrows.

"Are you putting your hand up, Atlas?"

"Yes." He tried to raise it higher without moving his arm from his side; but all that happened was that his fingers spread wide, as if he were a gecko trying to grip the sides of a wall.

"Have you hurt your arm?" said Ms. Balfour.

"No!" said Atlas, and he snatched his hand back down.

Now everyone was staring at him and he looked down. Ms. Balfour regarded him sharply for a moment, and then her eyes swept the class.

"Anyone else?" There were a few sniggers, and then, "Yes, Parjeet?"

As soon as the bell rang, Atlas threw on his parka and boots and ran to the little kids' side of the school where Peter waited to be picked up at what was called "the fort." This was really just a long snow wall that the grade ones and twos had been building all winter. On the days when there was no peewee practice, it was Atlas' responsibility to pick up his brother, and Peter liked to build while he waited.

"Hi, At—" said Peter, and before he had a chance to get out the words, Atlas grabbed him and rushed them away.

At home, his mother noticed the flowery smell.

"What's that?" she said, sniffing around him.

"Nothing," said Atlas, and then to his mortification, he felt himself prickling up with tears.

"Oh, sweetheart," said his mother, reaching for him; but he flung off her arm and ran to his room, slamming the door. He threw himself onto his bed and stared at the ceiling, hating the day and everything that had happened. When Peter came in, Atlas got up and went to the bathroom.

In the mirror, Tim Horton's strong, dependable face materialized. "Buddy, you look bad," he said. It wasn't an accusation or an exclamation, or even sympathy; just a fact.

Atlas nodded.

"What's going on?"

"Why am I so dumb? Tim, I don't know *anything!*"

"I doubt that's true," said Tim, "but why don't you just start at the beginning and tell me what's happening."

So, he did. He told Tim every single horrible and embarrassing thing. At the end of it, Tim said,

"Well, I guess you've got to pay Campbell back two dollars now."

Atlas nodded.

"And you'll need a bit more than that to get the right kind of deodorant."

"Yes."

"Your mom will get it for you if you ask her."

"No way."

"Félix could help."

"No."

"Well, how much money have you got?"

"If I break my piggy bank, I've got enough."

"It's a start. Atlas, welcome to the grown-up world."

Tim had gone. Atlas went back to his room and Peter had left again. He dug the fuchsia deodorant out of his knapsack and hurled it into the garbage. Then he got his piggy bank off the top shelf, where he'd been filling it up since before he was Peter's age; and, without a single thought or regret, he picked up Peter's fossilized rock from the window sill, shattered the piggy bank, and started counting change.

CHAPTER SEVEN

"It's Atlas' turn to choose," said his mom, coming in from the kitchen. She carried a big bowl of spiced popcorn, and Félix followed with a plate of cheese and veggies. Uncle Liron came last, inexpertly balancing a tray of drinks.

"*Tim Horton: Legends of Hockey*!" said Atlas.

Félix groaned.

"*Oye, amor*," said his mother. "It's Atlas' turn. Fair is fair."

"But, li'l dude," said Uncle Liron, setting down the drinks and hopping into the middle of the couch, where he crossed his legs, "you've seen that show a *hundred* times! What more's there to see?"

Peter, who was sitting in the frayed armchair at the window, turned a page in his book. "I like it," he said loyally.

"But, Vita—" Atlas' mother shot Félix a look that quelled him, and she grabbed the DVD from the shelf and put it into the player. The melancholy music started up, and the narrator said, "It's been more than a hundred years since those brave souls . . ."

Peter put down his books and came over to the couch. He crawled into Uncle Liron's skinny lap, and Uncle Liron smoothed down Peter's auburn coils so they wouldn't tickle his face. In colouring, Peter had taken after the father he couldn't remember, but Atlas was nearly as dark as all the rest of the Raphaels.

Félix and Liron started a quiet chat, and Atlas turned up the volume. Vita shushed them. Liron started to protest, but she said, "It's only twenty-five minutes for goodness sakes!"

Atlas let himself sink into the comforting words. "...more determined than any of them that he was going to be somebody . . . Timmy Horton, he was as strong as—I think he was Superman sometimes . . . Strongest guy that ever played in the National Hockey League, bar none. Thank god he was a nice guy! 'Cause he hated to fight." Atlas loved that. Tim Horton was a superman *and* a gentleman.

At the end was the part about the terrible car accident that had taken Tim's life at age forty-four. Atlas always felt sad that he had died and never had the chance to finish his amazing hockey career or see his girls grow up. He thought about Tim's words to him: *Don't regret things. Be grateful for what you have.* Was he thinking about his girls when he said that?

"*¡Excelente!* What's next?" said Félix, reaching for the dice on the video shelf. This was what they used to decide turns if there was an extra one—which there always was on Atlas' night. He always asked for *Tim Horton: Legends of Hockey* and since it was only twenty-five minutes long, they still got to have a full movie after. The high roll went to Peter.

"*Secondhand Lions*," he said.

"Yay!" said Atlas, but Uncle Liron slumped down and said, "Maaan, I was hopin' for *Cool Runnings*."

"Next time, baby bro, next time," said their mother.

Next to *Tim Horton: Legends of Hockey*, Atlas loved *Secondhand Lions* the most. He wished that, like Walter in the movie, he had an Uncle Hub and an Uncle Garth who could teach him shooting and fighting and give him a "what every boy needs to know about being a man" speech. But his dad was dead and the only uncle he knew was sitting right there in the middle of the couch, complaining that he had to wait to watch *Cool Runnings*. How could he grow up if he didn't have anyone to help him?

After the movie, when they were sipping hot chocolate and getting ready for bed, Peter said, "But they never said where Walter's dad is."

"Well, his mom's a single mother."

"Yes, like you," said Peter. "But I know where my dad is. Is Walter's dad dead, too?"

"I don't—"

"Nah, he's not dead, just disappeared" said Uncle Liron.

"Oh . . ." said Peter. "You mean, he just left his family?"

"Yeah—" but Uncle Liron clammed up at a look from his sister. He'd stepped into sensitive territory. Atlas knew this was about him and he knew that, after all this time, he shouldn't be so touchy about anyone talking about his dad; but he was.

Atlas looked over to the sideboard at the framed photograph of his father. Atlas was walking on his father's left side and Peter was toddling on his right, barely visible above the tall grass. They had all been in a field somewhere, walking away from their mother, who had taken the picture. Their dad rested one hand on Peter's head of auburn fluff and the other on Atlas' skinny eight-year-old shoulder. His mother must have called out, because his dad was twisting around and looking back with laughter on his face, his kilt mostly hidden in the grass, and his long, red dreadlocks flung out with the movement of the sudden turn, catching gold from the low-hanging sun.

Atlas had spent hours staring at the photo, trying to remember his father, trying to remember how that hand on his shoulder had felt. At first, he'd thought he could conjure it; but time had swept the memory of that touch and all the rest of his father into oblivion. Now, all he remembered were terrible feelings. Waiting and waiting at the window, taut with expectation; aching and aching with missing him, sick to his stomach; lying awake in bed at night devouring and devouring himself with yearning. He couldn't reconcile the happy face and kind eyes in the photo with all that pain. DVan Raphael, whose real name was Rory

McAdams, had taken his cool reggae name and his fancy reggae drums to Toronto and never came back . . .

Uncle Liron got up from the table, "Well, my turn to clear up," he said, and got busy in the kitchen with a clattering vastly out of proportion to the task, his arms going like windmills. Peter was nodding over his hot chocolate. His head slowly lowered to rest on his open book, and his chocolatey lips left a little brown kiss on the page. Atlas' mother and Félix went to sit on the couch, talking quietly.

"Pero tendrás que decirlos pronto, querida. Necesitan saber."

"Todavía, no, mi amor. Pronto. Solo es que . . . Es una grand noticia, mudarse a España. Tengo que escoger un buen momento."

"Sí, sí, claro—"

"What?" said Atlas, sitting up. Something had penetrated. "Who's going to Spain?"

His mother and Félix both turned towards him with surprised, guilty eyes.

"Atlas! You—you can understand Spanish?" said his mother.

"Well, you speak it all the time. You said it's big news. But *he's* going back to Spain," he jerked his head towards Félix, "we all know that, 'cause his job here is only for one year. So why is that big news?"

"Oh, dear. Atlas, sweetheart, this isn't the way I intended you to find out."

"Find out what?"

"I've got a job in Spain, honey, a real job, using my training, not waitressing or—"

"*You're going to Spain?* But what about Peter and me!" He shouted so loud that Peter's head popped up and Uncle Liron bolted out of the kitchen, with a trail of soapy foam spattering behind him.

"You're coming with me, of course!" his mother jumped up from the couch and dashed over to give him a very uncomfortably tight hug. "I would never, never, *ever* leave you and Peter behind!"

"What're you sayin'? You're going to *Spain*?" said Uncle Liron.

"Liron, help out here for a minute."

He put his hands up, "Okay, okay, yeah I know. We'll talk later."

"Yes, we will," said Vita sternly. Uncle Liron retreated to the kitchen.

Atlas pushed back from his mother. "You never even asked us!" he said accusingly.

"I'll explain everything—"

"Explain! Adults always say that, but they only tell you what's already been decided and what you have to put up with and they never explain anything at all!"

Félix came up and put his arm around Vita. "We *will* explain everything, we promise."

"No!" said Atlas, "I'm talking to my mom, not *you*!"

"But, things are changing, little man. We're all together now and we all need to talk."

"We're all together—what does that mean?" said Atlas, looking both furious and scared. "And I'm not 'little man,' I'm a *boy*!" He pushed past them and rushed to the bathroom and locked the door.

CHAPTER EIGHT

"Why does my mom have to be dating that stupid Félix? It's all because of him!"

"Hmm, have you asked her what she likes about him?"

"No, of course not!"

"You should. You might learn something."

"What? Why?"

"Well, buddy, tell me this: do you love your mom?"

"Yes. 'Course I do."

"Now, now, that's the kind of answer you'd give to a teacher. Do you really love her?"

Atlas looked down, feeling ashamed. He was silent, but Tim seemed in no hurry at all. Slowly, Atlas started to speak. "Tim, she's the best mom, really she is. She's so funny—you should see her when we play games. She makes all of us laugh so much that we start losing. It's like her secret weapon."

Tim smiled, crinkling up the corners of his eyes. He nodded, encouraging.

"And she's really smart. She knows about everything. If a documentary comes on TV, she'll know all kinds of stuff about it before we even start watching. It drives Uncle Liron crazy. He says it makes his head hurt thinking about how she keeps all that information in *her* head." Atlas chuckled, thinking about it. "And she's the prettiest mom of all my friends—it's not just me who says so. Campbell says it, too. And she's really tough. Oh, you don't ever want to talk back at *her*!" Now he laughed right out loud.

There was a soft knock. It was Peter.

"Atlas, can I use the bathroom pretty soon?"

"Yeah, I just need a minute," he called through the door. Atlas turned back to Tim; but Tim wasn't smiling any more. He looked very serious. "And you know how tough it is that she's been raising you and your brother on her own, right?"

"Yeah . . ."

"It's real hard raising kids all on your own—especially with practically no money. Well, that was a bit different, but it's my greatest regret . . ."

"What do you mean?"

"Never mind. About your mom, you said she got a new job."

"Yeah—in *Spain*!"

"You should ask her about it."

"*Why?*"

"How much do you think I loved playing hockey?"

"More than anything!"

"You're right about that. And I was lucky enough to get paid for it. Best job in the world."

"Yeah!"

"What's your mom's job? Right now?"

Atlas had to think for a minute. His mom had had a lot of jobs. "Oh—she's a courier driver. You know, delivering packages."

"Is she, now? She likes to drive?"

Atlas shrugged. "I guess . . ."

"What does she love best? Like me with hockey?"

"That's easy," said Atlas. "Languages. She speaks a bunch of different ones. Spanish, obviously, and French, and Arabic I think, and some other ones."

"Wow, that's pretty impressive!"

"Yeah, it is."

"Maybe you could take her out for Valentine's Day to show your appreciation; do something nice. Ask her about her new job and find out if it's something she really loves. And find out what she likes about Félix."

"I can't ask her about Félix!"

"Think about it, Atlas. Would someone as smart and good as your mom date somebody who wasn't decent?"

"But—!"

"Well, ask her about her new job, then."

"Okay . . . Yeah, I guess I could do that. I've got some money now that I broke my piggy bank. I could take her to Tim Hortons."

"Does she like Tim Hortons?"

Atlas was surprised by the question. "Well, a bit . . ." he said, not wanting to hurt Tim's feelings.

"No, buddy, you've gotta take her to a place *she* really loves. Not the place you want to go. You've gotta put yourself in her shoes and figure out what she likes."

"Oh."

"Yeah, it's hard work showing someone you care about them, but believe me, it's worth it. I wish—well, it's worth it."

"Yeah . . ." Then something registered. "Wait, Valentine's Day? I'm not supposed to be responsible for that!"

"Oh, yes you are," said Tim with a grin. "Now you'd better let your little brother in here before he pops," and Tim faded away.

Atlas threw open the door, and Peter dashed in. "You'll tell me everything after, won't you, Atlas?" he said all in a rush as he ran past.

"Yes, sorry I took so long." Atlas went out and shut the door. He was going to go to his room, but he saw his mom in the kitchen through the counter-pass doing some final cleaning up in the dim stove light. It looked as if Uncle Liron had gone and Félix was sitting in the armchair by the window reading the newspaper; she was working alone. It was true what he'd said to Tim: his mother was the prettiest; but she looked sad and tired, too. He went to the kitchen.

"Mom?" she looked up. "Can I take you out to Tim—I mean, Bean Planet for coffee after supper on Valentine's Day? Just you and me? I've got some money."

"Atlas!" she said with surprise and her face opened into a beautiful smile. "Of course! Just you and me. That'll be such a treat. I'll ask Uncle Liron to come and stay with Peter."

"Hey," said Félix from the other room. "On Valentine's? I was going to—"

"Too late, baby, I'm booked!" and she gave Atlas a good, long hug. Atlas saw his mother lock eyes with Félix above his head and he followed her gaze. Félix harrumphed a bit, but he looked pleased, too. Why? Atlas would never understand adults.

"Time for bed, *Salta*," she said, and gave him a kiss. It was his mother's nickname for him, his name spelled backwards, and in Spanish it meant *jump*. *Because you're just like a Jumping Bean*, she used to say. But she hadn't used that nickname for a while. His dad had used it, too . . .

"Good night, Mom." He heard Peter come out of the bathroom and headed towards their room to tell him everything Tim had said. Maybe Peter would make some sense out of it. But how could anyone, really? Everything was too confusing.

❖

At some point the next day, as he was wondering how much a Bean Planet outing would really cost and worrying about how he would have the conversation Tim suggested, Harper floated through his thoughts.

Harper! Valentine's Day! He felt sick.

I should get her something, he thought. Since Valentine's Day fell on a Saturday, they'd have a little party at school next Friday, and everyone would give everybody else Valentine's cards. You weren't allowed to leave out anyone, so everyone got nineteen cards. But he wanted Harper to have something extra. What, though? And how would he give it to her without his classmates knowing?

He got up and counted his piggy bank money again, even though he knew exactly how much was left after he'd bought men's deodorant. How much would he have left after Bean Planet? He had no idea what a girl might like, but he couldn't start figuring it out until he'd done some research.

Bean Planet wasn't far away. "Mom," he called, "can I go down to the Comix Box?"

"More comics?" she said laughing, and looked at her watch. "Let's see . . . Okay, if you're back before two. Don't forget we're going to Canadian Tire."

"Oh, yeah. Okay, I'll be back before two."

"Can I come?" said Peter. He wasn't into comics the way Atlas was; he just liked to be with his big brother.

"Sure," said Atlas. Peter's math skills would be useful for figuring out his expenditures. "He can come, can't he?"

"Yes. You've got your watch?"

"Yep."

"Set an alarm so you don't forget."

Five minutes later they were walking down Vernon Street in the bright sunshine, listening to the squeak, squeak of the snow under their Sorels. Their breath hung in front of them in congealed clouds. Peter pulled up his scarf to cover his nose. Atlas explained his mission to find out the prices of things at Bean Planet and make an estimate of how much money he'd need for Saturday, and then how much he'd have left. Peter seemed happy to be going to a coffee shop to only look and not buy, even though he'd thought they were going to the Comix Box.

Bean Planet was warm and fragrant, but it couldn't compare to Tim Hortons—and the prices were definitely higher! After spending some time trying to guess what their mom might want to get next Saturday, he and Peter decided it would be a good idea to reserve ten dollars. It was probably more than Atlas would need, but he'd be safe from a potentially embarrassing cash shortage.

"Are we still going to the Comix Box?" said Peter, pushing up his glasses.

"That's a good idea; maybe . . ."

"Maybe what?"

"I need to check out some comic book prices. Do you think girls like comic books?"

"I'm not sure Mom would," said Peter doubtfully, assuming they were still talking about her; he didn't know anything about Harper, and Atlas wasn't about to tell him. Peter wouldn't laugh at him, and he was good at keeping secrets, too, unlike most small children; but Atlas couldn't bear the thought of anyone else knowing about Harper.

"Let's go," said Atlas. They crunched down the street and into the warmth and musty smell of the comic shop. Where to even start? There were thousands of choices! He knew which ones *he'd* want, but he didn't have a clue now that he was searching for someone else. He kept thinking of Tim's words: *You've gotta put yourself in her shoes and figure out what she likes.* What did Harper like? Atlas didn't know.

After a few minutes, Atlas realized he needed to do some research. So, he prepared for the next week at school.

CHAPTER NINE

Practice on Sunday was gruelling—Coach had seemed much more like Mr. Wick than usual—but Atlas still took time getting ready for Monday. He went through all his comic books meticulously. He didn't have a large collection, but it took a long time to go through them, because he was now trying to see them through Harper's eyes, and that was very difficult. He finally settled on *Superman, Man of Steel: Reign of the Supermen 21*. It was one of his favourite comics ever. A comic book would be great as a present, because it was something he could afford. But first, the research.

So, on Monday morning, when he sat down, he left his comic book clearly sticking out from his binder. Harper sat down and he said hello to her brightly, and she grinned at him. His insides flopped. He put the binder right to the edge of his desk. However, Harper was busy getting pencils out of her case and she didn't look. The class was still getting settled, and it was noisy, so Atlas chanced a bit of conversation.

"Do you like comics?"

"What?"

He slid the comic book out further to show her. "I got this

Superman issue—it's *Reign of the Supermen 21*, my favourite one. Do you like Superman?"

"Super*men*?" said Harper. "I thought there was only one Superman. There can't be anyone else as strong as him, or else how would that work?"

Atlas' hopes plummeted. This was surely not the kind of question a comic book fan would ask.

Kelsey was leaning forward now, apprising the situation. "I like Supergirl," she said, "but I don't read comics much."

"Well, there are lots of superheroes, right—" Atlas started to explain.

"I can't keep track of them all," said Kelsey.

Harper wrinkled her nose and cut him off. "Superheroes. It's always just men saving the world."

"No, it's not, there are women. Do you like Superwoman—like Kelsey?"

"No, not really. I like the *Series of Unfortunate Events*. Do you read those? I'm on book nine right now."

"No, I don't read those. That's a lot of books! How many are there?"

"Lots. I think there will be thirteen because that's the unlucky number."

"Why?"

"You really don't know anything about Lemony Snicket?"

"Who? No."

"Well, they're great books and they *really* make you laugh! They have *lots* of hard words in them, too, but they're usually funny words, so it's nice."

"Oh," said Atlas, disappointed. He fell silent just as Mr. Wick walked up from behind and scooped up his comic book.

"You know the rule, Atlas, no comic books in class. And quite a bit less chatter, too, if you don't mind. Come and see me after class and I *may* give this back to you."

Atlas sighed inwardly. So, not comic books. That wasn't what Harper liked.

Tuesday, he showed Harper his vintage hockey cards, the kind that kids used to collect when his mom was little. He'd gotten them for Christmas two years ago. Most of them were cracked and dog-eared, but he liked looking at the names and profiles of the famous old hockey players from the seventies: Bobby Orr, Guy Lafleur, Pete Mahovlich—he knew all their names and numbers. Harper was more interested in the cards than the comic book, at least. She'd never seen them before. She examined quite a few, commenting on which players she knew and which she'd never heard of. Atlas glowed with pride. She liked his cards!

But when the bell rang, she handed them back and said, "I wonder when we're ever going to get a women's hockey team? I'd get *those* cards!"

"Hockey cards? What's that?" said Kelsey.

So, not hockey cards either. That was probably just as well, because he didn't know if he could get them by Friday, and he didn't even know how much they cost.

Wednesday was a gamble. After practice, when they'd gone to Tim Hortons as usual, Atlas saved his hot chocolate cup. At home, he washed and dried it, and then packed it carefully on top of the books in his knapsack so it wouldn't get crushed. He pulled it out and handed it to Harper.

"I saved it from last night. Do you want to roll up the rim?"

"Roll up the rim?" said Kelsey, leaning forward over her desk. "Let's see! Roll it up!"

"Okay." Said Harper, "But what if I win something? Won't you be a little upset?"

"Nah," said Atlas, far more nonchalantly than he felt. "Go ahead."

"I'll split it with you," said Harper, and she smiled at him. Atlas grinned back and he felt his whole face turn red.

"*Better luck next time*," read Harper.

"Oh, too bad."

"Do you know anyone who's ever won something?" said Harper, handing the cup back.

"Not yet," said Atlas, "but I have a good chance. I go to Tim Hortons a lot. Hockey teams like to go there after practice, you know."

"My team goes to Wendy's."

"Wendy's is better!" said Kelsey.

"Oh—but do you like Tim Hortons? Do you like Timbits?" Atlas had thought of Timbits because they weren't very expensive.

"Yeah, they're okay, I guess. I like the chili at Wendy's."

"Oh."

"ATLAS! Will you zip the lip, face the front, and start taking notes!" said Mr. Wick. He jammed up his glasses with one finger on the heavy bridge across his nose, a sign of exasperation that they all knew not to ignore. Atlas quickly opened his scribbler and tried to look like he was concentrating hard. So, not Timbits, either.

Atlas was starting to feel desperate. It was already Wednesday, and he still had no idea about what Harper liked. He knew that, traditionally, women were supposed to like flowers and boxes of chocolates. But did this apply to girls, too? Well, anyway, he couldn't afford those things.

He was so embarrassed about the whole process that he hadn't even told Tim. But on Wednesday after school, his desperation outweighed his mortification.

"You look real worried, buddy," said Tim.

"I am."

"Tell me about it."

"It's Harper—you remember I told you about Harper?"

"I do."

"I want to get her something special for Valentine's. The class party is coming up on Friday and that's only two days from now, and I have no idea what to get her." And he explained about his experiments with various really top-notch items to see how she reacted, and how she didn't seem to like any of them.

"Hmm . . . Tough nut to crack."

"And don't tell me flowers or a box of chocolates!" said Atlas, "That would stick out like a sore thumb at school and the other kids would tease me forever. And I don't know if she's that kind of girl—I mean, she plays hockey! And, anyway, I don't have enough piggy bank money for that kind of stuff."

"You've really thought this through," said Tim approvingly.

"I haven't been thinking about anything *else*!" said Atlas. "It's making me feel sick."

"Keeping you awake at night?"

"Yes!"

"I know. I know what that's like."

"What should I do?"

"I'll bet you already know the answer to that one, buddy, but I'll tell you anyway. There's only one thing you *can* do when you want to get a present for someone that they'll really like."

"What? What do I have to do?"

"Think, Atlas, you've been doing it already."

"Research?"

"No, no!" said Tim; then, "Well, in a way. But it's not like science. It's more taking the time to get to know a person and really listening to them and paying attention to what makes them happy and what upsets them. You've gotta get into their shoes."

"But, but," Atlas spluttered, "I only have till Friday!"

"That's a kicker, for sure," said Tim. "Still, the same rules apply, and then you make your best guess."

"But I can't just guess!"

"Even people who've known each other for a long time sometimes get it wrong with gifts," said Tim. "But if that other person is worth their salt, why, they'll see the effort and thought that went into it."

Atlas let out a long breath. This was definitely much harder than he'd anticipated.

Tim regarded him. "Are you gonna give up?"

"No," said Atlas, straightening.

"That's what I like to hear." And Tim faded away.

Atlas went to his room and sat on his bed, thinking hard. Peter, as usual, wanted to hear what Tim had to say. Atlas only gave him generalities so he wouldn't have to talk about Harper.

"Why do you think he appears to you—only you?"

"I don't know. But one thing I know is I can sure use the advice."

"Yeah," said Peter, doodling in his notebook. "We can use the advice."

Atlas sighed. He felt both warmed and fearful inside that Peter regarded all of Atlas' problems as his own, too. It was comforting for someone to believe in him so fully, but he felt utterly inadequate. One day, when Peter had problems like this, would he be able to help? The way things looked right now, he was sure to be a screw-up.

That evening, he asked if he could come with his mom when she went grocery shopping, something he would normally have detested. Félix offered to stay home with Peter and get him to bed on time. As soon as his mother became engrossed in reading food labels, Atlas slipped into the mall and ran down to The Book Slab. He went straight to the Junior Fiction section and found the *Series of Unfortunate Events* easily; they took up half a shelf, there were so many of them. And they weren't like comic books, thin and printed cheaply; they were proper hardcover novels with beautiful illustrations. He turned over book ten slowly to see the price tag. Oh, no! It was so much worse than he ever would have guessed! He definitely didn't have enough money for that. He went back to the grocery store feeling dispirited and pawed randomly through the DVD bargain bin. Everything here was only $1.99, so he could afford any of them. He picked up a copy of *Tremors*. He had seen this one time when he slept over at Campbell's; his mom would never have let him watch it if she'd known. He loved it. But did girls like scary movies? He had no idea what Harper liked!

This putting yourself in someone else's shoes was very hard.

CHAPTER TEN

On Thursday, Atlas had planned to ask Harper about her movie preferences, but Mr. Wick greeted him at the door with "Atlas, you've been distracted all week and you're falling behind. I want you at the front today." Atlas groaned. The dreaded Front Desk sat right next to Mr. Wick's, only facing the other way. You couldn't get away with anything there, not the tiniest thing; and meanwhile, you knew that everyone else was staring at your backside the whole time. He'd rather have had detention. First period was simply endurance: surviving ignominy.

But in science class, something happened that wiped it all from his mind. Ms. Klimt gathered them around an aquarium with a tight lid. Inside were numerous fat brown bugs with what looked like armour in sections and long, probing antennae. "Who can tell me what these are?" said Ms. Klimt; and Atlas found himself calling out at exactly the same time as Harper: "Madagascar Hissing Cockroaches!"

"Eww," said several people.

"Disgusting."

"You're a cockroach!" said Gavin Eccles, pushing Luis Lamenca, who pushed him back, crying, "You're a roach, cock!"

One girl, who had been hanging back, made a little squeak.

Ms. Klimt ignored most of this. "I see we have some Arthropoda fans among us," she said. "Buck up, the rest of you, they're only bugs. And unlike the cockroaches you may be familiar with, these ones don't run wild all over the place."

"That's what I told my mom," said Harper, "but she still wouldn't let me get one. She said they'd multiply and swarm all over the house."

Atlas laughed. "My mom said the same thing! Then she wanted me to get a fish. But who wants a fish? They're boring."

"A hissing cockroach will sit quite still in your hand when you pick it up. Who wants to try?"

Atlas threw up his hand and he noticed that Harper did, too. He beamed. But Ms. Klimt called on Travis, a burly boy with a strangely small, heart-shaped face. He put out his hand gingerly. Ms. Klimt lifted the lid of the aquarium, and those who weren't enthusiastic about bugs made a hasty retreat to the back of the pack.

"Simmer down," she said, placing the insect on Travis' palm. He flinched a little but held steady, and the brute sat still in his hand.

"Now, Tiny, come up here." Tiny was a gristly girl with short-cropped red hair, and her name was really Tyranna; but she was so small that everyone called her Tiny, including herself. She stepped forward.

"Let's see why this cockroach is called hissing," said Ms. Klimt. "Tiny, give that fellow a poke."

Tiny looked at Ms. Klimt with round eyes, but Ms. Klimt nodded. "Go on; give him a poke."

Tiny gave him a poke. The creature let out a long, loud clatter that sounded like a miniature semi-truck's hydraulics.

"Cool!"

"Do it again!"

"Let me see!"

"Eeew!"

There was a parting of the class, with some surging forward and others hanging back. Atlas noticed that Harper was right at the front, craning to see, and that gave him an idea.

After school, he dropped Peter at home, and then without even asking for permission, he ran down to Waldo Mall Place. It was quite a few blocks away, and by the time he got there, he was both cold with the freezing weather and sweaty from running in all his winter gear. He stepped inside Thump Bump pet store and pulled off his gloves and toque, shoving them inside his parka pocket. He knew Thump Bump pretty well. There were always too many people at the front with the puppies and kittens and rabbits, but that wasn't where he hung out. He headed over to the reptiles. He spent some time looking at the snakes and iguanas and watched a chameleon swivel one of its baleful eyes at him; then he went further back to the dark, restive corner filled with arachnids and insects. He went past the stick insects and leaf insects, and then the weevils scurrying over dead leaves and waiting to be scooped up and fed to lizards, and then mealworms squirming in great balls. His heart thumped. Would they have hissing cockroaches? They didn't always have them. Please, please . . .

There they were!

He looked at their shiny, sectioned bodies in amber and bronze and dark cinnamon, with little bits of soft beige and cream showing through at the sections, pulsing a little. Sitting placidly, magnificently. This would be a *wonderful* present that no one else would ever *think* of getting Harper. And if she got it as a Valentine's present, her mom could hardly say she couldn't keep it!

And then he saw the price on the side of the tank. Did they mean —no, it couldn't be! Not for a single one? That was almost as much as a hardcover Lemony Snicket book!

Atlas stood there, deflated, despairing. Tomorrow was Valentine's. What would he do? He looked up and down the row. Everything was so expensive! How had he never noticed this before? Well, the meal worms were cheap of course, but meal worms weren't a present. He wiped viciously at a tear that leaked out without his permission.

He felt in his pocket. He didn't need to count his coins; he knew them all by heart. What could he do with such a small amount? He paced and then his eyes fell on . . . Well, maybe . . . They were very cheap anyway; only ten cents each. Even with his small mound of change, he could get quite a few. And who didn't like *them*?

So, he made his decision. The clerk who boxed them up said,

"What're you feeding? Salamanders? Shrews? No, wait, let me guess —you're a mantid guy, am I right?"

"It's a surprise for someone," said Atlas.

"Ooh. And a tasty one, too!" laughed the clerk. "Maybe they're for you? Some people like 'em."

"They're not for eating!" said Atlas.

The clerk laughed. "Oh, I get it, a Chinese culture enthusiast!"

Atlas didn't know what that meant, so he didn't say anything. The man handed him the box. "Just keep 'em happy with lettuce leaves and apple cores." Atlas hadn't thought about what they ate, so this was useful information.

"Okay, thanks," he said, and he plunged the box into the inner pocket of his parka to keep it warm on the walk home.

That evening, he and Peter sat at the table filling out Valentine's cards for all the kids in their classes while their mother and Félix baked cookies for them to take to the party tomorrow. Atlas smiled to himself, because he had an absolute secret weapon present that no one else would have thought of, because nobody had paid attention like he had, and Harper was going to love it!

CHAPTER ELEVEN

Like always, the party was saved for last period. That was so the parents could deal with most of the sugar rush at home, Mr. Wick said. In English class, Parjeet had noted that since tomorrow was actual Valentine's Day, the fourteenth, that meant today was Friday the *thirteenth*, and wasn't that bad luck for a party? Mr. Wick told him to stop being ridiculous.

They then had a long lecture about the origins of Valentine's Day, and Mr. Wick made them write a one-page essay answering the question: *How is the original purpose of Valentine's Day reflected today?* Atlas couldn't see much of a connection between martyrdom and love, and the truth was, he hadn't been listening very carefully during Mr. Wick's lecture because he was excited about his gift for Harper. So, he made up some stuff about martyrs loving their enemies and that's how Valentine's became a festival of love.

At last they were told they could stow their books and put their desks into a big circle, and Mr. Wick went to get the treats from the staff room. When they circled the desks, their usual order got mixed.

"Dude, over here!" called Campbell, but Atlas said, "I'm going this way," and jostled hard to get his desk next to Harper's. But flighty, annoying Jolene, with her swinging ponytail and sparkly hair ribbons, had gotten in between. He tried to go to the other side, but Kelsey had already pulled up her desk there. So, he stayed put, and he had to peek around Jolene to try to gauge the best moment to give Harper her gift. As Jolene was very bouncy—up and down and sometimes even crouching with her feet on the seat and bouncing on her haunches—it was hard to keep track of what was going on with Harper. She looked so pretty, wearing a white blouse with narrow white seams all down the front, long sleeves covering her skinny arms, and a dark red ribbon at the collar. It was a lot girlier than the things Harper usually wore, girlier than Atlas liked, but on her it was beautiful.

All the cards were handed out and then the treats. Isaac was made to put back the two extra cupcakes he'd grabbed, and then no one wanted to take them because of how he'd mashed them with his grubby hands. He said he might as well take them, but Mr. Wick said being a swine was not about to be rewarded and threw them in the garbage.

It was nearly time for the buzzer, so, not having been able to determine a best time, Atlas leaned over to Harper and handed her the small box he'd wrapped in tissue paper. "It's a present for you, Harper!" he whispered. Harper looked surprised and pleased and started to tear off the paper. Oh no! He didn't want her opening his gift here and now—everyone would see, and it would be humiliating! He leaned around Jolene, who had nosily stuck her face right down to look, "Harper!" he whispered. Harper leaned behind Jolene's back to hear. "Don't open it till—" he had just started to say, when she tore off the rest of the paper, and the lid came with it in her hand.

There was frantic hopping and Jolene lurched back, screaming. Her head banged Harper hard in the face. There was a spatter of crimson, and Harper cried out.

"Get off her!" he said to Jolene and gave her a shove. Jolene stopped screaming and gagged, coughed, and Atlas saw a creature fly out of her mouth. She screamed again and then pitched forward and threw up all over Harper's desk.

The class erupted, and some people grabbed books and started smashing around trying to kill the hoppers. "Don't! They're just crickets!" cried Atlas. Several cupcakes sailed across the classroom. Harper leapt away from her desk. Her nose and lip were bleeding, and there was blood and vomit splattered across her white shirt. Atlas ran around Jolene.

"Harper!" he said, reaching out to her.

But Mr. Wick was there—or maybe it was really Coach, for he was calm. He had a wad of paper napkins grabbed off the treats table, which he shoved up against Harper's nose, obscuring most of her face. "Hold that tight," he said. "Nothing broken? Okay, good. Harper, get down to the washroom. Kelsey, you go with her. Jolene, why are you crying? Are you hurt?"

"A bug went in my mouth!" sobbed Jolene.

"Is it out now?"

"Y-y-yes!"

"Are you hurt anywhere?"

"N-n-no!"

"Then go with Harper and Kelsey and get cleaned up." Mr. Wick glanced up at Atlas hovering there and said, "Go get Ms. Hatwal, will you? Tell her we need a mop up." Ms. Hatwal was one of the janitors. Atlas wanted to go see if Harper was okay, but he dashed in the opposite direction towards the janitor's closet. He knocked on the door and there was no answer, and he could see through the little window that there was no light on. He realized he didn't have any idea how to find the janitor, so he ran towards the office. But turning a corner, he nearly skidded right into Ms. Hatwal, just finishing mopping up something spilled in the hallway.

"Whoa!" she said. "What're you doing out of class?"

"Mr. Wick sent me to find you. We need a mop up."

"Oh, Valentine's Day," sighed Ms. Hatwal. "It's a big mopping day. What is it this time? A pitcher of juice dropped on the floor?"

"No—at least—I don't think so. Cupcakes and cookies . . . And throw-up . . . And blood . . ."

"Ugh! I'm going to need more supplies. What has your class been *doing*? Easier to clean up than juice, but I don't know what is worse. Well, go tell Mr. Wick I'll be there right away."

Atlas rushed back to class, now feeling sick. He was going to be in such trouble once Mr. Wick got to the bottom of what had happened.

So, after class, a phone call was made to inform Atlas' mother that he'd coming home from school late, and he spent the rest of the afternoon on the unpleasant task of sorting the smelly contents of the lost and found bin—which at this time of year featured many moldering single mittens, frayed scarves, smelly insoles from winter boots, and laces encrusted with mud and salt. Peter couldn't go home by himself, so he had to stay at school, too, and he immediately jumped in to help Atlas, but was told by Mr. Wick that he couldn't; so, he sat and wrote in his notebook while Atlas worked. Atlas was even made to clean the bin itself, and then he had to endure a meeting with Mr. Wick, Ms. Martin, and his mom, in which he was told to explain himself. But how could he? He didn't know how things had gone so wrong, nor could he explain how Jolene had managed to get a bug in her mouth, nor fathom why Mr. Wick was so upset about the crickets.

"You released insects into my classroom! *Forty* of them!"

"But they're only crickets. They won't hurt anyone."

"*Only* crickets. You don't even seem sorry."

"I am!" So much sorrier than Mr. Wick could imagine. Harper would probably hate him forever now.

Mr. Wick jammed up his glasses with one finger and, forgetting the separation between himself and Coach, said, "You're off the next four games!" and he left the room.

CHAPTER TWELVE

At supper and all evening, Atlas said not say a word and his mother cast him worried looks. Peter slipped his hand into Atlas' under the table. Atlas couldn't even bring himself to talk with Tim. So, as soon as he was done with clean up after supper, he went to bed. He fell into a heavy sleep.

But much later, he woke up. At first, he didn't know why he felt so miserable, and then he remembered everything. He lay for a while, staring at the ceiling and replaying the day in his head—every single sickening moment. But, eventually, he couldn't stand it anymore and he got up. The glowing numbers on the alarm clock said 2:19 a.m. He went to the bathroom and locked the door.

In the eerie incandescence of the night-light, Tim was waiting.

"Buddy . . . What's going on?"

Atlas told him.

Tim listened, and unlike the teachers, he didn't interrupt and get everything mixed up asking irrelevant questions; and unlike his mother, Tim didn't look heartbroken. Atlas couldn't stand that look from her. Tim let him go until he ran himself out, and then they were both silent in the near-dark for a while.

"I'm sorry, buddy, that's one really bad day."

Atlas nodded. Then, after fighting against it all day, tears started to drop. Tim let him cry; and to his surprise, Atlas didn't even feel embarrassed. He just felt relieved.

Again, they stood in silence for a while.

Then, Atlas said, "But Tim, *why*—?"

"Whoa, let me stop you right there."

Atlas was surprised. "What's the matter?"

"Why. That's the matter."

"What do you mean?"

Tim took a moment to mull. Atlas could see him rolling thoughts around inside his head, his mouth tightly closed in a small knot, his long chin jutting out.

"Well, here's the thing. There are a lot of questions that start with 'why' that just can't be answered. So, when you ask those kinds of questions, you can drive yourself crazy."

"Like what? What d'you mean?"

"Okay, here's an example. Why does Peter love and look up to you so much?"

"'Cause I'm his older brother!"

"Sure, but plenty of people have older brothers they don't look up to."

"Well—I guess—because we don't have a dad and Peter wants some kind of, like, someone"—he couldn't bring himself to say *man*—"to, like, help him out, you know?"

"And . . . ?"

"And because . . . Well, I don't really know why. I don't know *why* Peter looks up to me so much! And it scares me, 'cause he treats me like some kind of hero, and I'm *not*!"

"Right. So, you could say it's a mystery."

"Yes. Yeah, I guess it is."

"And since it's a mystery, if you ask why, you can't get any good answer."

"But then, what'm I supposed to do?"

"Try this," said Tim. "Think about Peter and ask a question that starts with *how*."

"Okay. Well, how come—?"

"Whoa buddy, 'how come' is just another way of saying 'why'!"

"Oh . . . yeah . . . okay."

Atlas thought.

"How can I be a good brother to Peter? To help him grow up?"

Tim grinned a wide grin. "That's what I'm talking about! Do you see the difference? That kind of question gets you pondering about things you can *do*! Think of it this way. Remember when I got injured? If I'd sat around saying: *Why did this happen to me?* do you think I'd have had a comeback like I did? No way. I'd probably still be sittin' there looking at my bum leg and feeling sorry for myself. But instead, I said: *How can I get back on the ice as soon as possible?* Once I asked that question, I could think of all kinds of things I could *do* and just get down to work! Hard work is a lot easier than trying to find the answer to mysteries."

"Yeah, I think I get it. But how does that help me with Harper?"

"Well, let's think of a coupla good questions about that."

Atlas thought.

"Maybe . . . *How can I let Harper know what I was really trying to do?*"

"There's a start."

"But that's too hard!"

"Did you hear me complaining in rehab?"

"But that's different! It was only an injury. This is a *girl*—it's way worse!"

"Hmmm, you've got a point. Okay, think of another question."

"Umm—*How can I make it up to Harper?* I guess she had a pretty bad Valentine's Day, too."

"Good. Now, even if it takes some time, you can get down to work with things you can do."

"Yeah. Or—maybe: *How can I let Harper know that I care about her?*"

"That's a good question," said Tim. Then he started to fade. Atlas watched until the very last shadow of him in the mirror was gone. He almost felt peaceful.

But answering that question was going to be just about the hardest thing in the universe.

CHAPTER THIRTEEN

"This is such a treat," said his mother, and she shrugged off her parka and hung it over the back of her chair. Bean Planet had mismatched comfy chairs of all shapes and colours, unlike the simple, consistent seats at Tim's.

"What do you want, Mom? You can have anything you want."

"I think a cappuccino."

"Big or small?"

"Oh, a nice big one, please!"

"What about something to eat?"

"Hmm . . . I'm pretty full after supper, but I could just squeeze in a lemon square."

"Okay! You stay here and I'll get everything." Atlas went to stand in line. There was a very tall man in front of him and a *very* tall, broad woman came to stand behind him, holding a squirming child on her hip. Atlas was suddenly aware of how short and skinny he was, sandwiched between big people and not able to see what was going on around him. The line crawled. The toddler's snow-booted foot kicked out and hit him, and Atlas saw there was a big salty smudge on his sleeve. He moved forward out of range, but annoyingly, the large woman immediately moved closer behind him, and the child's chubby leg kicked out again. Now he had a salty smudge on the other sleeve. This went on until it was finally his turn to order, which he did in a rush. Then he had to wait for the cappuccino to be made. He didn't realize it took so long! This wasn't like Tim Hortons, where it took no time at all to get a hot chocolate and some Timbits.

He brought the tray to the table, walking carefully so that nothing spilled. His mom was looking very peaceful, reading a novel while she waited.

"Oh, look at this! You even remembered that I like cinnamon on top!"

Atlas beamed as he unloaded the tray.

"What've you got all over you coat?"

"Oh—" Atlas explained about the twitchy child and he brushed at it, but he knew salty dirt would never come off without a proper washing.

"Turn around. You even have it on the back of your head!" laughed his mother. "That kid must have been one kicker. Just like you, *Salta*, when you were little."

Atlas made a swipe at his hair. Well, he'd deal with it when he got home. "Try the lemon square," he said to his mom eagerly, "is it good?" and they got down to the business of sipping and eating. His mom tried some of his hot chocolate and a nibble of his double-chocolate-chip cookie, and she pronounced everything wonderful. Atlas grinned. This was nice, giving his mom a treat.

Then he remembered what Tim had said about being interested and asking about his mom's new job. Tim said to find out if it's something she really loved. Until Tim got him pondering, he had never thought about his mom's jobs or whether she liked them. He could remember her working as a security guard and a bartender and a ramp handler—whatever that was—at the courier place, before she got promoted to driver. She said she liked that a lot better, but . . .

"Mom, do you like your job?"

"What? Doing delivery? I like it well enough. Sometimes it sucks when the weather's really bad, but most of the time it's okay."

"But you didn't like being a ramp handler?"

"Not so much. It's assembly work. It's just full-on and you always have to be paying attention. You can't blink for a second or you'll miss something. It never lets up, which is stressful, but there's zero chance to use your brain or have some agency."

"What's that?"

"Like being in charge of something. Being able to make some choices. Some jobs don't have much of that."

"Oh." Atlas had never thought about this. "What about when you were a bartender? Did you get to have some agency then?"

"More than on the assembly line, for sure! You learn about mixing all kinds of drinks and you get to chat with customers, which is nice. I enjoyed the interaction with people."

"What about when you were a security guard?"

"Oh, that was *so* boring! Mostly just standing around, and then when you were interacting with people it usually wasn't so nice—either telling them off for doing something they shouldn't have, or else calming them down so you could go find a lost child. It wasn't for me."

"Oh." Silence. "I don't remember what you did before that."

"All sorts of things. Similar things."

"Did you have a favourite job?" Atlas saw his mother's eyes go very far away, and for a minute she looked sad. She didn't answer for a while, and then she came back from wherever she'd gone, looked at Atlas, and smiled.

"There was one job I really loved when I was in university. I got to work for a prof marking assignments he got from his language students. I liked helping the students do better, and it was like constant basics revision for me."

"But I thought you *were* a student when you were at university."

"I was, but at an advanced level. I was marking undergrads, which means they were just starting out; so, I could mark their assignments."

"Oh!" Atlas wondered about this amazing information for a moment.

"But why the sudden interest in my jobs?"

Atlas shrugged. "I dunno. I'm just curious." And then, trying to be very nonchalant, he said, "What about your new job? You know, the one in—" he couldn't bring himself to say it.

"In Spain?"

"Yeah. What's that job?"

Atlas watched his mother's face light up and then cloud over and then rearrange so quickly that if he hadn't been thinking about what Tim told him and paying attention, he would have missed it. "It's a teaching job."

"Teaching people Spanish?"

His mother laughed. "No, they already know how to speak Spanish there."

"Oh, yeah . . ." She made a goofy face and he laughed, too.

"English is the one language course I *will* teach. The other course, if I translated the title into English, would be something like *Critical Thinking and Ethics for Linguistics Research*—"

"I don't know what that means."

"No, neither do most people. And I get to do research."

"You mean—like writing essays?"

"Something like that."

"Oh. And that's what you want to do?"

"Yes, very much."

"More than delivering courier packages?"

"Very, *very* much."

Atlas didn't know what to say to this. When he thought about teaching, he imagined Mr. Wick, and he couldn't see his mother writing assignments on the board and standing at the back of the class making sure everyone was working and sending people to the principal's office . . . Though at a university, with adults, he supposed it might be a bit different. And he couldn't see what was fun about writing essays. But the one thing he *could* see was that his mother was lit up in some different way.

He thought back to what Tim had told him to do. *Ask her about her new job and find out if it's something she really loves.* It seemed it was. And then Tim had said, *Find out what she likes about Félix.* That was crazy! But maybe it was important . . .

He started to speak, and he meant to ask about Félix, but instead he said, "What did you like about Dad so much?"

"Your dad? Oh, Atlas, he was the most wonderful—he was so much fun, and he was a kind person; always so good to everyone. He had a way of accepting people. He had such kind eyes, he was so easy to laugh. And he was *dreamy* good-looking. That's why you're so handsome—"

"I don't look anything like him, though," said Atlas doubtfully. "Dad had red hair and freckles!"

"But your features and your kind eyes are exactly like his, Atlas."

"Are they?" he put a hand to his cheek.

"Yes. That's the funny thing! You came out dark like me, but you look like him; whereas Peter is light with that wild reddish hair, but his facial features and his build are 100% Vita! We got two completely different mixtures in you two boys. Your dad always loved that. And he was such a good dad. Not like some of his buddies. He wanted to be right there in the middle of the puke and the wailing. He walked the floors with you night after night. He was never happier than when he was cuddling you or singing to you or chasing a ball around with you. He always worked till the wee hours of the morning with his band, you know, and he'd be so tired when you kids got up, but he was always happy when you came and jumped on him."

Atlas tried to remember such cheerful times, but there seemed to be nothing before all the longing. "But—he left us!"

"The reggae scene in Toronto was always a lot bigger than here. The prospects were—well, he was never going to be able to make a go of it here. That's why he went to Toronto. We've talked about this before, don't you remember? The plan was that once he had a stable foothold, we'd join him. I couldn't chance leaving my job before then. We thought three months, if we were lucky . . . then it stretched into six . . . and then the accident . . ."

"Why did he go there? He shouldn't have gone away!" said Atlas, and he was angry that tears had sprung up and spilled onto his cheeks.

"Sweetheart . . ." his mother reached out a hand towards his, and he leaned away.

"And if you loved Dad so much, how can you let Félix—"

"Hi, Atlas!" said a voice. He and his mother turned. Harper was walking towards them, her lip puffed up. The tiny, dark ends of stitches poked out.

Atlas jumped up. "I have to go to the bathroom," he said to his mother and fled. Behind him, he heard his mother saying, "You must be in Atlas' class at school. I'm sorry, he's just gone to the washroom."

Atlas was acutely aware of the salty mess along both his sleeves and even on the back of his head—and worst of all the tears. Had Harper noticed? And what would she think now that he'd run away? He stood in the bathroom for a long time, grateful that no one came in.

She would hate him after this.

CHAPTER FOURTEEN

Peter didn't like playing hockey on teams, but he liked playing with Atlas, who never body-checked him and who taught him how to skate properly. So, Peter was delighted when, on Sunday while the rest of the peewee team was at practice, Atlas walked with him down the street to Fleury Close and the neighbourhood rink. They had the place to themselves, so first they did circles around the ice to warm up, and then Atlas said they should practice cross-overs. Peter wasn't good at cross-overs, but he wanted to be; so he tried gamely, skating with his weak ankles turned in. He fell again and again.

"Come on, Peter, up, up!" Atlas called, and Peter would scramble up.

Then Atlas said they should practice stick handling and hugging the boards—just like Tim Horton—but as there were no boards, the puck kept flying off into the snow banks.

"Can we play hockey now?" said Peter after a while. His glasses were all steamed up.

"Okay. I'll play net and you try to score."

"Yay!"

It was easy to stop Peter's shots, but Atlas let a couple in so his brother wouldn't feel too bad. Atlas wondered if this was good older brother leadership, or whether he should be harder on Peter, like Coach was with him and his teammates at practice; but he couldn't see the point. Peter was never going to be good at hockey and he was never going to be on a hockey team, and it would just make him feel discouraged.

After a while, Peter said he was getting cold, so Atlas helped him get his skates off in the little shelter. He loosened the laces where Peter's numb fingers only fumbled and pulled them tighter, and held Peter's Sorels, first one, then the other, for him to push in his frozen, clumsy feet.

"I'll see you back at the house later," said Atlas.

"Okay," said Peter. "How much longer are you going to stay?"

"I dunno. A while. I want to keep up with my skate drills so when Coach lets me come back, I won't be rusty."

"That's a good idea. Do you want to play *Top Trumps* after?"

"Maybe. We'll see." Peter loved that game because of all the stats he learned. He didn't really care if he got the top score; but Atlas wasn't as keen, top score or not. "Not *Dinosaurs* again, though."

"*Predators?*"

"Maybe. Or *Super Heroes and Villains*, maybe."

"Okay." Peter headed home, and Atlas watched him down the block, which was the rule. Then, once he'd seen Peter go in the apartment building door, he circled the ice—circled and circled. It felt good to just skate. The tepid winter sun slid towards the horizon. and the sky turned from robin-egg blue to dark cobalt with a thin rim of deepening peach. It was nearly dark when Campbell appeared. Atlas gave him a stick salute but kept skating, and Campbell sat down at the shelter, laced up, and joined him. Atlas didn't ask him about practice. He didn't want to know.

They spent some time passing the puck back and forth, something Atlas couldn't do with Peter, and then they tried to steal the puck from each other. It felt good, pushing himself against Campbell, willing himself to master his friend's bigger bulk. After a while they slowed down, gliding and circling. Campbell was so smooth on the ice—so at home. When he was skating, there was hardly any twitching at all. Atlas wished he could skate so well.

"Did you talk to your mom about Spain?" said Campbell.

"A bit," said Atlas, not looking up.

"Are you really moving there?"

"I dunno. I guess so. Mom seems really excited about her new job."

"Man, you can't just move away! How long will you be there?"

"I dunno," said Atlas. He hadn't asked his mom this question. He was scared of what answer he might get.

"Do they have hockey there?"

Atlas stopped dead, and Campbell skated into him.

"Dude!" said Campbell.

"I—I don't know. Félix never . . . I never asked Mom." How could he have failed to find out? Surely, they must have hockey there. Surely!

Campbell skated slowly around him. "Do they have snow there?"

Did they? Atlas ransacked his memory for things he had learned about Spain at school or on TV, but he couldn't dredge up anything. He stood, feeling dread. His mother wouldn't move them to a place with no hockey, would she? She couldn't!

"I'm half frozen," said Atlas. He'd been on the ice for a long time. "I've got to get home."

They headed to the shelter and tugged at stiff laces with half-dead fingers.

"How come you hardly talk to me anymore?" said Campbell.

"What?" said Atlas, absently. He was trying desperately to remember anything that either his mother or Félix had said about hockey in Spain.

"Like just now," said Campbell. "You're not talking to me, you're just staring."

"What? I talk to you."

"No, you stare off into space like you're on some other planet."

Atlas kept his head down.

"I dunno . . . I just, I'm just thinking about a lot of things. I really don't want to move to Spain."

"Yeah. It sucks."

"How can she just decide that and not tell us?"

"Adults are always doing that."

"It's not fair."

"Why do they do that?"

"I dunno. Adults are stupid. I never want to be like that," said Campbell.

"But we have to become adults," said Atlas.

"Not yet."

"Like Tim Horton," said Atlas.

"What?"

"When I become an adult, I want to be like Tim Horton. A gentleman. Strong as an ox so you couldn't put anything over on him, but fair and fun and a gentleman."

"I guess," said Campbell. "I never really thought about it."

They slung their skates over their shoulders and stumped down the street on numb feet. Atlas said goodbye to Campbell at the Candler house and carried on to his apartment building. His body hurried him forward with single purpose to get into the warmth, but his mind was flitting from one thing to the next like an anxious bird, lost in the inky sky.

CHAPTER FIFTEEN

Félix hadn't known if there was hockey in Spain, but he said, "I never heard of people playing hockey. But maybe . . . It doesn't mean there isn't any. I've just never been into hockey, so I wouldn't know."

That wasn't encouraging. Atlas knew that if hockey was unpopular or a new sport in Spain, then it wasn't likely it would be available for children.

"Is Valencia a big city?" asked Atlas. He knew, also, that big cities were usually best served.

"Oh, yes," said Félix. "It's Spain's third city, very cosmopolitan. If there is hockey in Spain, it will be in Valencia."

Atlas felt cold and fearful that he knew nothing about this city his mother was taking them to; he wasn't even sure he could find Spain on a map. "I have to know!" he said. "Mom, can I go on the internet to find out, please, please, please, *please*!"

"No," she said. She was unyielding about computer use. "But I'll go on the computer with you after supper."

"Right after supper?"

"Yes! Now let's eat."

Atlas started to gulp his food and Félix said, "Atlas, please, manners! And perhaps some appreciation for what your mother has prepared."

"Chew it at least," said his mother. "We don't want to be doing the Heimlich maneuver."

"Oh, I read about the Heimlich maneuver," said Peter, and launched into a detailed technical explanation. Atlas saw Félix roll his eyes, but his mother laughed and gave Peter's hand a little squeeze. Then she reached past Peter and patted Atlas on the shoulder.

"Right after dinner," she said, "don't worry." Atlas realized that his mother knew how important hockey was to him. He had never thought about that before. She had always got him all the equipment he needed, of course, and signed him up for teams and made sure he had rides, and even watched as many of his games as she could when she was off work. But it had never occurred to him that she thought about what was in his heart—that longing for hockey which he couldn't explain, even to himself. These thoughts amazed him, and he stopped eating.

"You're not choking, are you?" said Peter, shaking him. "Can you speak? If you're choking you can't speak."

Atlas roused himself. "No, I'm not choking," and he continued eating, slowly now. He was wondering whether he had the same depth of sympathy towards his mother as she did for him. Their conversation at Bean Planet was the first time he had ever asked her about her own thoughts and feelings. That she had an interior life separate from his own now loomed up before him: a powerful, new, inscrutable truth.

After dinner, Atlas' mother got up and went straight to the little desk in her bedroom where the computer lived, and Atlas followed. It was an old computer, and Atlas fidgeted while it wheezed and they waited for it to boot up.

They learned that the first ice rink in Spain was built in 1920. That seemed hopeful; but the Ice Palace, as it was called, was a place for fancy ladies and gentlemen to go skating for leisure. It wasn't a sports arena. There were restaurants and a coffee house and a cigar room and even a room for an orchestra—but!—an ice hockey game had been played there as part of the opening night entertainment! So, there were people in Spain who knew hockey, and there had even been a league and a championship series some years later. But then there was a long gap in the information, and they couldn't find more.

"Maybe the wars changed things," said his mother.

"What wars?"

"Well, the two World Wars, but there was also a terrible civil war in Spain, between the World Wars." They kept searching. They came upon some recent clips and news about hockey. There was a video.

"Click it! Click!" said Atlas. A man came on screen talking in Spanish very rapidly. Atlas got only a few words. Then the camera panned to the game behind him and—

"That's not hockey!" said Atlas, indignantly. "There's not even ice! They're not even on skates!"

"In-line skates, it looks like," said his mother.

"Roller skates," said Atlas disdainfully.

"But you can see they're playing the same game, the same rules."

"That's not hockey!" shouted Atlas, and once again, he felt himself on the verge of tears. He pushed them back and ran out of the bedroom and into the bathroom, where he stood panting, trying to master his emotions.

He sensed he was being watched. It was Tim. Tim looked at Atlas but said nothing; he just waited. Atlas turned away, but after a minute he said, "How long have you been there?"

"Since you came in," said Tim.

"Oh."

Silence.

"Well, aren't you going to start quizzing me like adults always do? What's wrong Atlas? You look upset Atlas. Tell me what's going on Atlas."

"I guess you'll tell me what you want to when you want to," said Tim.

More silence.

"Well if you need to know, *everything's* wrong! They don't even have hockey in Spain!"

"They don't? I didn't know that."

"No, just sissy in-line skating around on a wooden floor. It's no fair that I'm going to have to leave hockey."

"That's the truth."

"And—and—" Atlas looked at Tim's strong, peaceful face. "Lately I've been crying, Tim, *crying*! Why can't I stop?"

Tim considered. "Well, buddy, I don't think you'd want to."

"Yes, I do! It's terrible to cry in front of other people!"

"Embarrassing, why yes. But crying is human. It's just being a human being. So, you don't want to erase it, trust me."

Atlas' chin jutted out. "Oh, yeah, easy for you to say! You're super big and tough and *you* don't cry."

Tim looked grave. "You're dead wrong about that, buddy. I've cried a lot of times. Don't you think I bawled like a baby when there were family troubles?"

"What family troubles?"

"I wasn't always a good father. I was away a lot, and when I was home, everything revolved around hockey and me and my career. The girls had to tiptoe around the house and be quiet as mice so I could get my sleep before games."

"But it was important. You had games, NHL games. You had to play your best so you could win the Stanley Cup, and you couldn't let your team down."

"Yes. Yes. But they needed a father . . ."

"What're you saying? I don't understand."

Tim looked sad and he gave a great sigh. "There *are* things more important than hockey," said Tim, and when Atlas was about to protest, he cut him off. "But what I'm saying is: in any family, there are puzzles that can't be solved. If I'm going to be the best hockey player I can be, I have to be away from home nearly all the time and be single-minded and focused at the expense of everything else, and I'm not a good dad. I'm neglectful, distant. And if I want to be a good dad, I need to be available and spend time with my girls, and then I'm not a good hockey player. A puzzle that can't be solved. I don't know if I did the right thing or not."

"You did!"

"Yet it doesn't feel like it. I still *remember* hockey with the same passion I always had; but when I think about my girls, I *feel*. It's all feeling, all raw."

Atlas shook his head against the confusion, and then a thought arrested him: "Do you think it was like that for my dad? With his music I mean?"

"Yeah, it mighta been."

"D'you . . . D'you think it's like that for my mom? With her languages—that something inside is driving her? Like hockey was driving you?"

"It could be. But I can tell you one thing for sure. All this time, she's been choosing to be here for you kids rather than playing her own game."

"But now?"

"All I can tell you, Atlas, is to pay attention. And be curious. And trust your mom. Anybody can see that she loves you boys more than the sun and stars."

CHAPTER SIXTEEN

No matter how much he was dreading Monday, it came anyway. He didn't want to face Harper with her swollen lip and her memory of him running away with tears streaking his face; and he dreaded that Mr. Wick might still be so angry that he would make Atlas sit at the Front Desk, with everyone's eyes burning into his back.

He breathed a sigh of relief when Mr. Wick said nothing as he flopped down into his own desk. He slouched down and tried to make himself small. Maybe Mr. Wick wouldn't even notice he was there. Harper came in and sat at her desk across the aisle from him. Her lip looked even worse than it had on Saturday—still swollen, but now purple and green as well.

"I'm sorry about your lip," he mumbled.

To his surprise, Harper gave him a lopsided grin—keeping the part with the stitches immobile so only one side of her mouth curled up. "It looks like I got a real injury in hockey, doesn't it?" she said.

"Yeah, like the puck hit you in the face mask. Does it hurt much?"

"Not too much anymore, as long as I don't bang it or eat hot stuff."

"Oh, well that's good. I bet it hurt getting the stitches."

"No, the doctor froze my lip first so I couldn't feel it. But what *really* hurt was getting the needle to freeze it! That made tears squirt out like crazy." She splayed out the fingers of both her hands in front of her face several times to show how the tears had squirted. Atlas looked down, wondering if she was thinking about Saturday and *his* tears. His face burned.

"That sounds horrible," he mumbled.

"Anyway, it wasn't your fault, it was that stupid Jolene, sticking her nose in like a big snoop."

"I'm sorry all the crickets got away."

"Yeah, it would've been cool to have crickets at home. I could've kept them in the old turtle aquarium. I wonder if Pebbles was still alive if he'd eat them?"

"I dunno," said Atlas, trying to remember if he knew anything about what turtles eat. "I wanted to get you a hissing cockroach, but . . ." He trailed off, realizing that he had nearly embarrassed himself by admitting to not having enough money and buying Harper a cheap gift instead. Liking a girl was perilous!

"Really?" said Harper, her crooked grin hitching way up. Atlas forgot about trying to be invisible to Mr. Wick and sat up straight.

"Enough chatter!" said Mr. Wick, "Quiet, Parjeet, and put away that book! We're reviewing figurative language today. Who can tell me what that is?"

Mystified glances went all around the class. Atlas looked over to Campbell to see if this made sense to him, but Campbell was sitting drumming quietly on his desk, and seemed quite unconcerned with figurative language.

"Come on, come on, we covered this only a few weeks ago. Scour the insides of those brains. Surely they can't be completely empty!"

They scoured their brains, and the day began. Atlas couldn't concentrate at all because he was thinking of how Harper had smiled at him . . .

He carried the memory of that smile with him through the day, like a secret weapon he'd been given, a secret that no one knew about but him. He wanted to tell Campbell, but he didn't know how, so he didn't say anything.

But at lunchtime, Campbell said, "What's up?"

"What do you mean?"

"You look like something's up. Oh—I know! You found out about hockey in Spain. They have peewee hockey there, right?"

For several hours, Atlas had forgotten all about his bitter disappointment of the previous evening, and a sudden panicky feeling returned. How could he have forgotten? Reading his face, Campbell said,

"They don't?"

"No. All they do there is stupid hockey in a gym with in-line *roller skates*. There aren't any teams for kids!"

"No way!"

"Yeah. Félix says I should think about soccer, because that's what everyone plays there—only they call it football."

"That's lame. Man, that's terrible."

After that they bad-mouthed Félix specifically and Spain in general for a while, and then they tore out some pages from their scribblers and played several rounds of battleship. They were evenly-matched, and the series ended in a draw because lunch was over before they had time to play a tie-breaker.

Atlas spent the rest of the day yo-yoing between despondency when he thought about giving up hockey, exhilaration when he remembered how Harper had smiled at him. and then again wretchedness when he remembered that, in a few months, he'd move to Spain and Harper would forget all about him. He'd probably never have a chance to ask if he could walk home with her or go to a hockey game together, or maybe even hold her hand. He flushed thinking about it.

But all that evaporated when he went to pick up Peter. He headed to the snow fort, expecting to see Peter there in the darkening afternoon compressing snow blocks. But turning the corner, Atlas saw the broad back of Jimmy Zimlinski, his arms pumping, and he heard a small voice crying out.

Atlas dropped his knapsack and pelted forward, shouting, "Get off him!" He rammed into the bigger boy with the best body check he could throw and then felt himself bounce backwards, his breath knocked out of him. Peter cried out and Atlas jumped up, shouting. He rammed Jimmy Zimlinski again.

"Get *off*!"

"You get off, pinhead," said Jimmy Zimlinski, and he turned and flung out his arm sideways so that it bashed Atlas hard in the side of the head. Atlas was protected somewhat by his toque, but it still made his skull jangle and knocked him onto his haunches. He jumped up again and he saw Peter wriggle free and start to run away, but Timmy Zimlinski grabbed him.

"Let me go!" Peter yelped.

"Sure, I'll let you go," said Jimmy Zimlinski, and he pushed Peter face down into the snow. Peter's glasses went flying and Jimmy Zimlinski swiped them up.

"Give me those!" shouted Atlas, fury pumping through his limbs. He put his head down and rammed Jimmy Zimlinski again, and then he battered him with his fists with all his strength. He heard Peter scuffle up and get knocked down again, and there was a crunch and more scuffles. Atlas couldn't see around Jimmy Zimlinski, but he kept pummeling, and then he felt himself being dragged back and heard angry adult voices, and the blood was coursing through his head so that he couldn't hear what anyone was saying.

"Peter!" he called, and he felt the weight of his little brother rocket to his side and hold onto him tight, and he put his arm around him, and they were being pulled into the school.

The damage was this: Peter's face was streaked with tears and he had an ugly scrape down his cheek where he'd been thrown to the ground, but otherwise he seemed okay. However, his glasses were broken, having been first snapped in two by Jimmy Zimlinski and then trampled in the scuffle, so that one lens had a spider-webby crack through it. Peter held them forlornly in his lap and blinked, looking around with his short-sighted eyes. Atlas was still too angry to feel any pain, but he thought he was okay, though his head would probably hurt later. He didn't know if Jimmy Zimlinski was hurt in any way. He couldn't see how he would have been—he was too big and strong and well-padded in winter gear—but Atlas hoped he'd managed to inflict something, *something*. The three of them were sitting outside the principal's office and the boys' homeroom teachers had been called. Ms. Crampon looked very upset.

"Oh, dear, dear, boys. You can't solve things with fighting. Jimmy, Jimmy . . ." And she left it hanging. Atlas supposed Jimmy was in the office every other day. He looked at the older boy's bulky body, hunched in the chair opposite, his eyes staring ahead as if they were turned off, as if there was nothing behind them at all.

Mr. Jacinto appeared first, looking concerned and stooping to look at Peter's face and ask him how he was. A minute later, Mr. Wick came in looking agitated. "Atlas!" he said with an accusing tone —which Atlas thought was extremely unfair, since he didn't even know what had happened yet. Then Ms. Albertson hurried in. Peter was asked to explain everything. He told them how he had been building the wall and Jimmy Zimlinski had walked over and started pushing it down for no reason, and how Peter had asked him to please stop the random destruction, and how this had seemed to enrage Jimmy Zimlinski, and how things had gone berserk after that. Because Peter was such an articulate child, they got a detailed account of events, and all the while, Jimmy Zimlinski sat silent with his eyes turned off.

"Why did you push over the fort?" said Ms. Martin to Jimmy; but she looked as if she didn't really expect an answer, and there was none. She gave a great sigh. "Come into my office please, Jimmy." Jimmy complied, letting his arms dangle as if he wasn't the one controlling them, and Ms. Albertson followed, looking disheartened. Before shutting her office door, Ms. Martin turned to Atlas and said. "As Mr. Wick is your homeroom teacher, I'll turn him over to you."

Atlas supposed this meant that Mr. Wick would send him and Peter home; but he was wrong.

"Atlas, what's going on with you lately? Your head isn't in your schoolwork—that stunt you pulled on Friday—and now fighting!"

"I wasn't fighting," cried Atlas, "I was protecting Peter!"

"With your fists. That is not acceptable. Why didn't you call a teacher?"

"Peter was getting beat up right then! I wasn't going to leave him to get a teacher!" How could Mr. Wick not understand this?

"Fighting is for hooligans, and it's not allowed on school grounds." Then, disregarding the demarcation between himself and Coach for the second time in less than a week, Mr. Wick said, "You're off peewee practice for four more games."

Atlas was speechless, and in the shocked silence, Mr. Wick left the office, glowering.

Atlas felt a small hand slip into his. "I'm sorry I got you kicked out of hockey," said Peter.

"You?" said Atlas. "It wasn't you! It was that *piss*head Jimmy Zimlinski and that *ass*, Mr. Wick!"

"Language," reproved Ms. Crampon—but as if her heart wasn't really in it.

"Let's go home," said Atlas, and he and Peter gathered up their mittens and toques. Atlas put his arm around Peter's shoulder, and with his heart thumping leaden and full of confusion and shame he thought, *How am I ever going to become a man like Tim Horton that no one can push around and be a gentleman, too, if I can't even protect my little brother?*

CHAPTER SEVENTEEN

"Why can't I be strong like you? Then I could have just put my arms around Jimmy Zimlinski and squeezed, like you used to do to your hockey opponents, and then he would have had to stop. Why do I have to be so—so—puny! And skinny!"

"Buddy . . ." Tim waited while Atlas worked out his frustration by punching a stack of towels. Then there was silence for quite a long time.

"D'you remember what I said before about *why* questions?" said Tim.

Atlas looked down. He nodded.

"Are you ready to think of some good, helpful *how* questions?"

A pause. A nod.

"Then, let's do it, buddy."

Atlas looked Tim square in the eyes—those calm eyes, small in that big, rectangular face and bordered at the top by an unruly fringe of eyebrow loping crookedly from one temple to the other, and with deep, long smile creases fanning out on either side.

"How . . ." Atlas tried to think of a how question, and his mind was blank. Then he was distracted by something. He leaned forward, peering with his nose up close to the mirror. What colour were Tim's eyes anyway? He couldn't tell, and then he realized that Tim was black and white, just like the old photos of him in books. Atlas stepped back. Had he always been black and white? He thought back, raking his memories, but he didn't know. How could he not know this?

"What's up, buddy? You look confused. You all right there?"

"I—I—you," he began, then mumbled, "I must be going crazy."

"Now hold on. Stop that negative talk. That's not how a champion thinks."

"I must really be losing it," said Atlas louder now, and struck by how ludicrous this situation was, locking himself here in the bathroom every day, talking to Tim.

"What *are* you really?" said Atlas. "A ghost? How come you don't have any colour? How come nobody else sees you? How come I don't see you anywhere else? Like in the washroom mirror at school?"

Tim chuckled. "Well, those are a lot of *how* questions, even if it's not really what I had in mind. But I guess it's possible you could see me somewhere else. I don't think it would be at school, though. That's not very private."

"Yeah . . . It'd be really weird trying to have this kind of conversation with a bunch of kids going in and out. Plus, they'd totally freak out!" Atlas laughed at the thought of it. But he quickly sobered. "Am I going crazy, though? Really?"

"No, you're not," said Tim, firmly.

"Yeah, but it's *you* telling me that and you're dead. So that doesn't really make me feel better. *Are* you a ghost?"

Tim looked thoughtful. "No, I wouldn't say that. More like . . . An essence."

"What's that supposed to mean?"

"It means it's hard to explain," said Tim. "But let me ask you this: whatever I am, do you trust me?"

"Yes," said Atlas immediately. It was true.

"Why? How do you know you can trust me?"

Atlas thought. "Well, it's just that . . . You always give me good advice. Sometimes I don't like it, but then I know that it'll help me. It'll help me figure out what to do or how to be better."

"Okay. So, if that's the case, maybe it doesn't matter so much exactly *what* I am. What's more important is that you can depend on me."

"Yeah. Yeah, I guess that makes sense."

"All right, then, back to what's getting you all twisted up: let's cut it down to size. What's a good *how* question you can ask about it?"

"How . . . How . . . *How can I protect Peter?*"

Tim nodded encouragement but said nothing.

"How—can I do a better job?—no, that's not it. Maybe it's better . . . *How can I help Peter protect himself?* 'Cause I might not be there when something happens, right? So he needs to know what to do. But he's *really* small. If I'm puny, *he's* a midget—even for a six-year-old. What can a kid like him do against someone like Jimmy Zimlinski?"

Atlas thought. If you were really small, the best you could hope for was to be super fast so you could get away in time, or invisible so you wouldn't get noticed, or have big friends who would protect you, or have some kind of superpower. But Peter wasn't fast or invisible and he didn't have any friends that Atlas knew about, and he definitely didn't have a superpower. Well, he *was* a genius, but that didn't seem to be a superpower that helped you avoid bullies.

Then a new thought occurred to Atlas: *why* didn't Peter have friends? He was kind and peaceful; thoughtful; generous towards others. Wasn't that a kid anyone would want to be around? So, why didn't he have friends?

Atlas had a sudden feeling that Peter must be terribly lonely at school, and he was gripped with a kind of yearning he'd never felt before—a yearning not from his own heart, but on behalf of someone else. And it was so vast that it almost felt like a physical ache. Atlas put his fist to his chest and rubbed.

Tim waited.

"How—?" Atlas whispered, then stopped. "He needs more than just a big brother. He needs friends. How can I help him?"

Tim nodded and replied in a voice so soft that it was almost tender: "Now, that's a damn good question."

CHAPTER EIGHTEEN

As usual, Peter wanted to know everything Tim had said to Atlas, and as usual, he sat peacefully drawing in his ever-present notebook, looking as if he wasn't paying any attention; but Atlas knew that afterwards, if he asked, Peter would be able to repeat everything back to him. Only this time, Atlas didn't tell him everything. He didn't want Peter to worry that *he* was worrying about him. After a while, Peter put down his pencil and rubbed his eyes.

"This is giving me a headache," said Peter. "I'm gonna go see if it's time to set the table yet."

After dinner, it was Peter's habit to sit at the table and do Atlas' homework with him. Grade ones didn't have any homework, but Peter was always interested in what Atlas was learning. Atlas wasn't a fan of homework. Having Peter there made it more tolerable—and if he was honest, Peter often helped him figure out things, especially math things, when he got stuck. But tonight, Peter got out their collection of locking-blocks and built castles and moats and trebuchets. After a while, even that was taxing for his eyes and he said he was tired and went to bed. Atlas could see the concern in his mother's face as she went to tuck him in.

Homework was a lonely endeavour without Peter, and it seemed to take forever.

It was hard to concentrate, and Atlas kept getting distracted by his mother's and Félix's voices in the kitchen. They were talking about Peter.

"It's going to take time—you can't just get them off the shelf," his mother was saying. "He has such an unusual prescription and the lenses have to be ordered from Germany. What's he going to do in the meantime, not being able to draw or read? And I'm not sure what they'll do with him at school. I'll have to go see the teacher. I wish I could just keep him home—take him tobogganing and skating—keep him busy."

"Maybe Liron could take him?" said Félix. "Classes are in recess all this week. Probably, I could make some days off the coming week."

"I'd hate to ask Liron. You know how he's struggling with his courses. He really needs the study time."

"But send Peter to school?'

"I don't know. I could kick myself that I didn't get a second pair of glasses for backup. But they're so expensive! I don't know how I'm going to manage."

"It should be the parents of Jimmy Zimlinski paying for those glasses," said Félix.

His mother let out a long sigh, and to Atlas' surprise, her next words were, "Poor Jimmy Zimlinski." Atlas sat up. "That kid doesn't stand a chance with his family. He'll probably run away from home when he gets a little older, and then I shudder to think . . . The poor kid has some serious learning disabilities, but he's not dumb . . . Only, with his family situation and his behavioural issues, he just can't seem to . . . It was probably Peter using such big words that set him off. This little grade-one kid talking like a grown-up. It probably sounded like taunting to Jimmy."

Atlas had forgotten about his homework. His thoughts were rushing, and he strained to hear. Félix said something in Spanish that Atlas didn't know, then:

"*Amorcita*, we'll manage it together. The expense cannot be an issue when it comes to Peter's well-being. And when you have your new job, you'll no longer have such worries. You'll have proper pay! You'll be able to take him directly to Germany for his new glasses, if you want to."

For the second time that day, Atlas was seized by new thoughts. Jimmy Zimlinski wasn't dumb? And he acted the way he did because his home was terrible? And Mom wasn't able to pay for Peter's glasses? Atlas hadn't known that Peter's glasses were expensive or that they were so unusual they had to be made in Germany. And what about his mother's job? He already knew that she loved languages and had figured out that she probably hated her courier job—even though she never complained—but he had never thought about how much money she earned or that it might be difficult for her to afford the things they needed. He knew that peewees and all his hockey equipment were expensive, but he'd never thought it was a hardship for his mother. She had never, ever hinted at it! How had he not noticed these things? And now he was suspended for eight—eight!—games, and her money was going to waste.

He didn't know what he could do about that and he was positive, at least, that he didn't deserve the second four-game suspension. But maybe he *could* do something for Peter. He got up and went into the kitchen, feeling nervous.

"Atlas!" said his mother, putting her arm around him. "Done your homework already?"

"No, but I need to talk to you."

"Oh, Sweetie, it's not your fault about Peter. You did all you could!"

"I—" he found he really didn't want to talk about it. "It's not that. It's just that, I think Peter really needs to go to school. I mean, I know he can't see and he doesn't need to do the schoolwork. But he needs to be with his friends."

Inside, Atlas was trembling. He didn't know if this was the right thing. Peter didn't have any friends; but he never would if he just stayed home. So, Atlas was just going to have to figure out some way to help him.

CHAPTER NINETEEN

Their mother booked the day off to take Peter to the optometrist for new glasses. "It'll only take a couple of hours," she said, "but if I've got to take time off, why not make it a whole day and spend time with my favourite munchkin?" Peter looked delighted and Atlas was relieved that today he wouldn't have to worry about hustling over to pick up Peter before anything happened to him in the schoolyard. It surprised him to realize that a part of him was happy he wouldn't be going back to peewee practice anytime soon. That meant he would go get Peter every day, and he'd get there a lot faster than Félix ever did when it was his turn to get Peter on the peewee days. This realization filled him with a strange, dispirited wonder. He never imagined anything would make him happy to miss hockey.

Atlas could not have told anyone what happened in his classes that morning. He was preoccupied with new ideas from the day before. At lunchtime, deep in thought, he found himself sitting at a table with his lunch before him and no one else there. He felt a jostle beside him.

Harper had sat down at the table. His heart thumped.

Kelsey and Tiny sat down as well.

"What about Mr. Wick this morning?" said Harper. "He was so nuts!" and she jumped up and did an imitation of him patrolling the room with his arms folded, straightening his sweater, then jabbing at his glasses, then peering over peoples' shoulders and clearing his throat. Atlas broke into laughter, and Kelsey and Tiny went into gales of giggles. It was exactly like Mr. Wick.

"And you were like—" she sat down and hunched over the table like Atlas did when he was trying to concentrate on his work. She scratched the back of her head, making her hair stick up in a mess, hunched some more, messed up her hair more. Kelsey and Tiny howled.

"Do I do that? I mean, scratching my head like that."

"*All* the time!" she said. They laughed and Atlas joined in.

"Really? That's mental."

"Do me," said Tiny; and then turning to Atlas, "She can do anybody."

Harper immediately made herself seem to shrink and become small and made her eyes big and round. It was Tiny to a tee. Then she did both sides of a very clever Gavin Eccles and Luis Lamenca routine—for they were always together. Harper said you couldn't do one without the other.

"Guess who this is," said Harper. She stuck her nose right down to the table peering at something and then reared back and mimed throwing up.

"Jolene!" they all shouted. Then Harper mimed Jolene finding all kinds of unpleasant things—under the table, in her armpit, in Kelsey's hair—and every adventure ended with invisible vomit spewed everywhere. They were all laughing so hard that their sides were aching. It was the first moment that Atlas hadn't been mortified about the Valentine's Day party. Atlas saw Campbell come into the room, scan, and spot him. He put up his arm and waved.

"Th-there's C-Campbell," he gasped, hardly able to speak for laughing. Campbell headed over.

"Campbell!" said Harper, and went into another mime, now drumming the table, twitching her head, and blinking her eyes, and they all howled with laughter. Atlas saw Campbell freeze, then a look of horror clouded his face. He rushed out of the room.

"Campbell!" called Atlas, laughter suddenly dead within him. He ran after Campbell. He saw his friend's back whip around the corner. "Campbell!" But Campbell didn't stop. Atlas rounded the corner and saw the door to the library swing shut. He grabbed it, pelted through, then skidded to a stop, knowing that he'd be kicked out in short order if he ran or shouted there. He prowled the aisles, looking up and down, calling in a whisper: "Campbell! Campbell, where are you?"

Then he saw him, hunched in a dark alcove, looking strangely small.

"Campbell!" Campbell turned away. Atlas came and sat beside him. "Campbell, I—"

"Oh, you think that's really funny, making fun of me? D'you think I don't know that kids laugh at me behind my back all the time? But I didn't think *you* would, too!"

"No, they don't!" Atlas scrambled through his memory searching for verification of this. He couldn't remember kids making fun of Campbell—or maybe they didn't do it in front of him because he was Campbell's best friend? But why would they mock Campbell?

"I know what they say," contradicted Campbell. "I s'pose you get a big laugh behind my back saying it, too!"

"What do they say? I don't say anything behind your back!"

"As if! I saw you guys."

"But Harper was just—"

"Making fun of me."

"No! It wasn't like that. She was doing imitations of everyone—Mr. Wick, Tiny, Jolene. She did me, too!"

"Yeah right. I know what goes on. Twitchy, retard, lame-brain. I know my mom is worried I'm turning into a Tourette's nutcase, but I'm *not*!"

"What's Tourette's?"

"Oh, yeah, act innocent. Just piss off."

"But Campbell! It wasn't—I don't—we were just laughing about everyone."

"Piss off."

"Cam—" but he was cut off by Mr. Beedle, the librarian, looming in front of them.

"There's far too much noise here. Atlas, out."

"But—"

"Out. Now," and he pointed towards the door.

Atlas got up, casting Campbell a worried look, but Campbell didn't look at him. Indeed, he didn't look at Atlas for the rest of the day. Campbell came in late to science class, but Ms. Klimt didn't say anything and only carried on showing them how to catch water bugs and transfer them into a petri dish for study. Campbell hung back, and when Atlas tried to circle around to stand next to him, Campbell moved away. It was the same in drama class. And in language arts during last period, Atlas tried to catch Campbell's eye so many times that Mr. Wick made him sit at the Front Desk.

"I want nothing but complete silence for the rest of class," said Mr. Wick. "*Complete* silence. The only thing you should be doing is working on your book report, and that does *not* require talking." Mr. Wick was so wound up these days that everyone complied immediately. Facing the front wall and not being able to see anything behind him, the silence was eerie. He imagined everyone's eyes drilling into his back. There was the sound of pencils scratching on paper, and the occasional sigh or desk creaking, and the soothing sound of—

"Crickets!" burst out Mr. Wick. "Those vile—they're driving me around the bend!" There was laughter, but Mr. Wick snarled so angrily that it died quickly. There had been no sign of crickets in the room, but clearly, at least some of them were still there, behind shelves and hidden between books and papers, or perhaps in cracks in the ledges and baseboards.

At last the bell rang. As soon as class was over, Campbell rushed away and was gone before Mr. Wick had finished giving Atlas one final lecture on his recent appalling behaviour.

Campbell was gone and there was no Peter to pick up today; Atlas was alone.

CHAPTER TWENTY

"I don't know how to explain to Campbell, but I have to. I have to let him know . . . It wasn't on purpose. We weren't trying to be mean. *I* wasn't trying to make fun of him. I have to tell him that. I don't know if he'll believe me, but it's the truth. I have to tell him I'm sorry. I'm really sorry."

"I can see that. Well, you know what to do, Buddy; you know what to do."

❖

A wind was blowing snow down from the mountains and the temperature was plunging. Peter thought school might be cancelled tomorrow, but Félix laughed.

"They never cancel school here!" he said. "At least—not for weather which, in Spain, we would say is unliveable."

"They *might*," said Peter. Atlas realized that he was hoping for another day with their mother.

"It's going to blow over before then," she said. "Anyway, come hell or high water or blizzards, I've got to be back at work tomorrow."

Atlas watched Peter deflate a little, but he held in his disappointment pretty well. Grade one was certainly not necessary for Peter academically, who long ago had surpassed all the schoolwork in his grade and the next and maybe several others above that; but their mother said it was good for him to be with children of his own age. And if he didn't have any friends amongst those children . . . Then what? Atlas wondered whether Peter was dreading going back to a place where he felt lonely all the time. His chest clenched up with worry, but he didn't know what to do about it. Right now, though, he *did* know something he needed to do.

"Mom, can I go to Campbell's house for a minute? I need to tell him something."

"In this weather? It's wicked out, Atlas. Stay inside and be warm and dry."

"But this is something—I need to talk to him. It's something really important."

His mother measured him with a sharp look; then after a moment: "Okay, but be back in fifteen minutes. Dinner's almost ready."

"I'll be back on time!" said Atlas, flying to the entryway to throw on his parka.

"Set the timer on your watch."

"Okay, okay!" He jammed on his boots.

"I want to see it!"

"I'm doing it now," he said, holding up his wrist to show her. Then he pulled on his mittens and rushed out the door.

Outside, the wind whipped the breath straight out of his lungs, and he dragged his hood up over his toque, the fake fur halo protecting him. He pulled his scarf over his mouth and nose and walked quickly, his boots squeaking on the hard-packed snow. The sidewalk, which had been clear earlier, was now completely covered again. He looked up to the streetlights, where snow flashed in white streaks as it drove past the coronas of light. Then he was at Campbell's house. Before he could be scared off by his own nerves, he punched the doorbell.

Nothing happened, and he realized his stiff mitten hadn't made any impression on the frozen button. He pulled off his mitten and tried again. This time, he heard the familiar ding-a-long-ding-ding sound inside Campbell's house, distantly. He waited, straining for footsteps, and pulled his mitten back on. He hoped it would be Campbell who answered.

The door opened, and warmth and golden light streamed out.

"Atlas!"

"Hi, Mr. Candler, is Campbell there? I need to—can I speak to him please, for a minute?"

"It's suppertime, Atlas. You should be home."

"Yes, but, it's important," he pleaded. "Please?"

"Well, let me see. Come in and I'll find him. But be quick; we're about to sit down for dinner."

"I'll be quick," said Atlas, and he stepped inside, closing the door behind him. He pulled off his mitts and threw back his hood, and within a minute, went from flash frozen to *sous vide*. He seemed to wait for a long time, and then he heard footsteps coming back—but not Campbell's. Mr. Candler reappeared.

"I'm sorry, Atlas, he says he doesn't want to talk right now."

"Oh. I—oh. Well—but," his eyes pleaded with Mr. Candler. He wanted to say, *Go back and tell him. Tell him I really need to talk to him! Tell him I'm really, really sorry!*

"Are you boys having a falling out?"

Atlas' throat was dry, and he couldn't reply. He pulled on his mittens. "Well, I have to get home. For dinner," he said, and he left, barely aware of the worried look on Mr. Candler's face and oblivious to the stinging snow in his eyes as he walked against the wind.

CHAPTER TWENTY-ONE

They were nearly late to school the next day because they were having so much fun sliding in the snowdrifts that had blown up overnight. The familiar, exciting feeling of a warm chinook was in the air, and they whooped and jumped and unzipped their parkas because they were too hot. As they got close to the school, the roads were all properly cleared and, therefore, fringed with ragged grey snowbanks spewed up by the snow plough, with ice chunks sticking up along the tops like broken teeth. These weren't so fun to jump in, so they walked in the middle of the road where the sun had melted everything clear and dry.

"Peter," said Atlas, "who are your friends at school?"

"You!" said Peter.

"Besides me."

"Campbell!"

"I mean friends your own age—in your own class."

"Oh. I don't know. All the kids are my friends."

"But who do you hang out with at recess?"

"At recess? Nobody. Usually I'm busy doing things that the other kids don't want to do."

"Like what?"

Peter shrugged. "I don't know. Like . . . Like maybe figuring out how long the school fence is or making a map, or—"

"What about building the fort? Don't you do that with other kids?"

"No, they do it during recess, but I do it after school."

"Why? Why don't you do it with the other kids?"

"It's easier. There's too many of them swarming around and they don't know what they're doing, so I wait until after school."

"Then, who do you talk to at school?"

Peter shrugged. Atlas stopped, and Peter walked on for a second before he realized Atlas wasn't with him.

"Atlas?"

"Peter, you've got to have some friends at school—friends besides me and my friends."

Peter sighed. "Yeah, I guess. I know that's what Mom wants, but I just don't . . ."

"You must have something in common with *somebody*," said Atlas. "Think about it. Whoever you have something in common with, try to make friends with that person. Like me and all the guys in peewee. We all love hockey, so it's easy to be friends."

"Okay," said Peter, looking doubtful.

"Okay!" said Atlas, feeling he'd had a good moment with Peter, being a good big brother. He was really helping.

But after school, when he went to pick up him up, Peter was working by himself on the fort as usual—except . . . A big figure loomed up from behind the wall and bashed a block of snow onto the top of the wall. Jimmy Zimlinski! Atlas broke into a run.

"Hi, Atlas," said Peter. "Jimmy and I are building the wall together. I'm packing the blocks and he's really good at adding them, especially since the fort's so high now, so we make a good team. Look how much we've done today!"

"Peter!" said Atlas, panicking. Was Jimmy about to burst into a rage again and start pounding Peter? But Jimmy and Peter both looked quite calm. "We gotta go!"

"Okay," said Peter, and climbing out from behind the wall he said, "We'll work on the wall some more tomorrow. See you, Jimmy."

Jimmy grunted and carried on hoisting up blocks.

"Peter!" said Atlas, as soon as they'd put some distance behind them. "What's going on? How did you get left alone with Jimmy again?"

"I asked Jimmy if he wanted to work on the fort with me."

"What? But why?" spluttered Atlas.

"Jimmy likes the fort a lot, so I thought we could work together. You said I should find kids I have things in common with."

"Yeah, but I meant—Peter, I meant kids your own age!"

"Well, Jimmy and I love building the fort in common, so why shouldn't we do it together?"

"But—what if—weren't you scared?"

"Not too much. I didn't think he was going to jump on me again. Something ticked him off before, but what are the chances the same thing would happen again?"

"Mom said it was probably because of the big words you use, and it made him—what did she say? She thought it made him feel dumb or something."

"Mom's right what she says about Jimmy; he's not stupid."

"She says that?—she said it before?"

"Yeah, she says that."

Atlas was dumbfounded. He couldn't remember his mother ever talking about Jimmy Zimlinski before. What else had he never noticed? Was he really that bad at paying attention? For a minute, he was lost in these thoughts as they walked.

Then he said, "Peter, promise me you won't build the fort with Jimmy Zimlinski anymore."

"Why? We both like building it. We should do it together. Anyway, I can't make Jimmy Zimlinski stay away from the fort, so that would mean *I'd* have to stay away, and that would be no fun."

Atlas sighed. He realized that school was probably so boring for Peter, and the other students were probably so far from being able to relate to him, that building the fort after class was the one thing he could look forward to each day. How could he tell Peter to stay away? But equally, how could he keep Peter safe? Peter might be a genius, but he was still very young and there were a lot of things he didn't know about life. He was far too trusting.

So, when they got home, Atlas made a beeline to the bathroom, filled with anxiety. He paced in tight circles around the tiny room.

"Why did I never notice that Peter has no friends?"

. . .

"Why, of all people, that Jimmy Zimlinski? It's not safe!"

. . .

"Why are there never any other little kids around when I go to pick up Peter?"

He stopped.

"Oh . . ."

Tim had been silent through all this, just watching. "What've you cottoned onto, buddy?"

"It's the parents! They're all waiting for the grade ones before class is even out. So, as soon as the bell rings, all the other kids are gone in a whisk."

"A whisk? Oh, you mean in a flash. Whisked up in a flash."

"Yes. And Peter's left waiting for me because our class gets out half an hour later. And Jimmy Zimlinski will always be hanging around, because he *never* goes home until they make him. He never hangs around on the big kids' side of the school where he should be because nobody likes him."

"Poor kid's got a rough school life and worse at home, eh?"

"That's what Mom says," said Atlas, in surprise.

He paced some more, chewing his lip and coming to a reluctant conclusion. "There's only one thing I can do, then."

"What's that, buddy?"

"It won't really matter . . . since I'm not in hockey anyway right now . . . and nobody comes over to the little kids' side of the school anyway, so nobody will see me . . . And no more messing around with friends after school . . ."

Tim waited.

"I'll just have to run over there as fast as I can . . . I'll have to get permission. Not from Mr. Wick. Ms. Martin, she'll understand. I'll leave last period early every day and *I'll* build that fort with Peter. He'll be happy, then. He'll be safe. It'll be worth it if he's safe."

"Y'know," said Tim, regarding Atlas thoughtfully, "I really don't think you even need me." And he grinned.

CHAPTER TWENTY-TWO

Atlas had to admit that Ms. Martin was a very reasonable school principal. It wasn't what he wanted, but it was a good enough compromise.

"I won't give you permission to leave class half an hour early every day, Atlas. You can see how that would be disruptive. You can have ten minutes. Peter will be fine on his own for twenty minutes, and then even if you're delayed a bit, you'll get there before Jimmy Zimlinski."

"Okay. Thank you, Ms. Martin."

She scrutinized him. Atlas fidgeted in his chair, wondering whether he was dismissed, and then she said, "I agree with Peter that it's unlikely Jimmy will be set off by the same thing again. And I agree with you that it's best to take no chances. It's not the kind of arrangement I'd have preferred, but it's the best solution anyone has come up with so far. I respect that you're trying to help your little brother. But please, take into account that this will disappoint Mr. Wick—"

"But—"

"It's unavoidable; just don't make a big deal of it. Don't create waves."

"Oh . . ." Atlas hadn't given any thought to Mr. Wick, apart from the fact that he was not the right person to ask for permission. "Okay. I won't make any waves."

"Good. Then scat. You've got about sixty seconds before the bell rings."

Atlas didn't have to be told twice. He didn't want to start the day by aggravating Mr. Wick.

It was a fidgety day. Atlas was tormented by the rupture with Campbell, and Campbell was still avoiding even making eye contact with him. Then there was Harper. She was being friendly to him now, which he'd been wishing for desperately; but it was confusing after the Valentine's Day fiasco, and her attention flustered him, and somehow being friendly back made him feel he was being disloyal to Campbell. He was so agitated that he was once again threatened with the Front Desk. So much for not making waves!

At lunchtime, Campbell was nowhere to be seen. Atlas went to the library and checked the gym, the washrooms, and the special resources room, but he couldn't find him. He drifted back to the lunchroom and Campbell wasn't there, either. Atlas scanned the roiling space, feeling how strange and overwhelming the lunchtime tumult was without someone to share it. He found a deserted table in a back corner and opened his lunch bag. A Kritter Kube turned itself on and cried out in a piercing, baby voice: "Feed me! Quick! I'm reaching hunger critical!"

Peter. Atlas grinned. The Kritter Kube was an obnoxious digital pet that his mother would never have let in the house on the basis of several important ethical principles; but Peter had won it at a birthday party, so it was allowed.

A birthday party, thought Atlas, that Peter had attended because *all* the grade ones were invited, not because the other boy had been Peter's friend.

Atlas' smile faded, and he shoved the Kritter Kube into his pocket. He nibbled half-heartedly at his lunch, wondering if Peter ate alone over at the little kids' wing. Was this how Peter felt at lunchtime? Why had he never thought to ask Peter who he ate lunch with? His eyes scanned the lunchroom and fell on Jimmy Zimlinski, another lone eater. A new, disquieting thought emerged. Was Jimmy lonely? Was *that* why he was so mean? It was certainly true that hardly anyone ever hung out with him, so it was hard to imagine he *wouldn't* be lonely; but that was because he was so mean. It was like a snake eating its own tail, a puzzle that couldn't be solved.

That day, and on Friday, too, Campbell refused to talk to Atlas. Atlas began his routine of leaving last class ten minutes early and joining Peter at the fort, and it was soon clear to Atlas that this was the highlight of Peter's school day. He was always watching for Atlas, waving him over. They worked together, Peter chattering happily until Jimmy Zimlinski showed up a few minutes later. Jimmy was a silent worker and Atlas had nothing to say to him; so, once Peter had chirped, "Hi, Jimmy!" things went quiet. Without hockey, there was nothing to rush away for, so Atlas began staying longer before finally insisting they go home. Jimmy was always still working mutely when they left.

"What do you do in school, Peter?" said Atlas. Most of the residents along the street apparently hadn't had time to clear their sidewalks today, and his and Peter's boots crunched in tandem in the churned-up snow.

"Just reading practice and phonics and worksheets and—"

"No, I mean, what do *you* do. That stuff's way too easy for you."

"Sometimes I work along," said Peter, "if the worksheets are nice. I can colour them and add my own pictures. I make mind maps out of them sometimes. And sometimes I read my own books. Mr. Jacinto doesn't mind. But not now. The only thing that doesn't give me a headache is building the fort. I can't wait till I get my new glasses!"

"Yeah, me too. But isn't it boring sitting and reading your books while everyone else is doing other stuff?"

"I *like* reading, Atlas!" said Peter.

"Yeah, I know, but . . ."

"If I don't feel like reading, sometimes I work on my brain attic."

"What's your brain attic?"

"It's from Sherlock Holmes—"

"What's that?"

"He's a detective in mystery books from Victorian times."

"Like from the 1800s?"

"Yeah."

That sounded boring; but Peter continued with enthusiasm. "Sherlock Holmes is a genius and can remember everything he ever comes across and in one of the books, he explains it to Dr. Watson—that's his partner. He says he doesn't take just any lumber into his attic, but only those things that are important and useful and then he organizes them all so that everything is in its place and easy to find when you need it."

"Oh."

"The lumber and other stuff represents ideas you keep in your brain," said Peter.

Atlas thought about it for a moment. "So that's what you're doing when the other kids are learning reading?"

"Yep."

"Oh." There was nothing else to say, because Atlas couldn't fathom what was going on inside his little brother's big brain. And he was sure there would never be another grade-one kid with much in common with Peter.

They walked the rest of the way home in silence. It was a silent kind of weekend. There was no hockey, and Campbell didn't come to join Atlas at the neighbourhood rink. Peter couldn't see the puck, so there was no point in taking him out to practice. They spent most of their time building lock-block structures—it was one of the few things Peter enjoyed doing that didn't bother his eyes too much. Atlas knew Peter missed his books and he offered to read to him, but he couldn't make sense of Peter's current astronomy book.

"How about I read comics?" said Atlas.

"But I can't see the pictures," said Peter.

"Oh, yeah . . ."

"It's okay. I think I'll make some stuff out of Waxxi Stix."

Atlas wandered out to the living room. His mother and Félix were talking quietly in the kitchen.

"I had to get a second pair so he has backup—I can't let this happen again. But cats in hats!—this is taking a chunk out of my finances!"

"Well, soon you will have a proper salary so these things need worry you no more. *No te preocupes.*"

"Yes, thank god for that. It's such a big move, taking the boys to Spain, so disruptive for them, but it really feels like things coming together, too. I think it's the right thing to do."

"Why do you keep second-guessing yourself, *amorcita*? Of course it's the right thing!"

Atlas heard his mother let out a long sigh, and he sighed, too. Moving to Spain. It loomed so large that he couldn't really grasp it. He didn't like to think about it. Until recently, he'd never given a thought to the financial responsibility his mother shouldered caring for him and Peter on her own. Now he found himself worrying about it. He went to the bathroom and stood in the dark without turning on the light.

"I guess it really is right . . . ?"

"What's right, buddy?" said Tim.

Another sigh.

Silence.

"Why do I have to worry so much all the time?" said Atlas; and he left the room.

CHAPTER TWENTY-THREE

Monday was bitter, with wind pelting hard snow pellets down from the mountains. When Atlas arrived at the fort, Peter wasn't there.

He must have decided it's too cold, thought Atlas, and he headed inside to Mr. Jacinto's classroom.

"Oh, it must have just missed you," said Mr. Jacinto, collecting up stubs of broken chalk from the chalkboard ledge. "I sent a message down to Mr. Wick's to let you know that your mom picked him up a short while ago."

"Is he sick?"

"No," Mr. Jacinto smiled, "his new glasses are in, and she's taken him to have them fitted. Peter is *very* excited."

"Oh! Thanks, Mr. Jacinto," and Atlas sprinted away. Some good news, at last!

Outside, icy wind pummeled him. He pulled his scarf up over his mouth and nose, and ice crystals formed on his eyelashes. He leaned into the lashing and walked with his head down.

A horn toot made him look up. A car was pulling alongside him, and the front window rolled down.

"Hop in," said the woman. "It's no day for walking. I'll drop you off before I go pick up my husband."

Atlas stepped back, thinking of stranger danger, and then a familiar head with messy hair poked around the woman's shoulder from the back.

"It's us, silly!" said Harper.

"C'mon, get in before we all freeze," said her mom, rolling up her window.

"Oh—thanks!" Atlas headed towards the back door, but Harper's mom called,

"Other side—the back's full!"

Atlas ran around to the front door on the other side and jumped in, seeing as he did so that Harper was sitting in the back between a toddler strapped into a car seat and kicking it with a dirty boot, and a boy of around eight with hair sticking up in every direction and freckles nearly obscuring his face. They must be Harper's younger brother and sister.

"I'm Mrs. Desjardins," said Harper's mom. "I guess you know Harper, and this is Brodey—" jerking her thumb back towards the freckled boy, "and this one's Jada. Harper says you're Atlas. What's your last name, Atlas-from-Harper's-class?"

"Raphael."

"Nice name. Where's it from?"

"It's Jamaican. It was really Am-Raphael, but my mom shortened it to Raphael to make it easier."

"It's got a nice ring to it."

Atlas felt strange and conspicuous sitting in Harper's car with her whole family in it—sitting in front, where Harper would be looking at the back of his head. His head felt very big and odd. He tried to think of something to say.

"So, you're the oldest in your family, too," he said, twisting around so he could see Harper.

"Oldest and boldest!" said Harper.

"Oldest and moldiest!" said Brodey with a shove.

"Piddle in the middle!" said Harper shoving back.

Well, that wasn't very successful. Atlas thrust his hands into his pockets, where he discovered the Kritter Kube that he'd shoved in there days before. He pulled it out and turned it over in his hands, fidgeting. The skirmish unfolded behind him.

"Pea-brain!"

"Half-wit!"

"Don't you two start, or it's buckwheat pancakes for dinner!" said Mrs. Desjardins. It suddenly went quiet, except for Jada shouting, "Yay!" and Mrs. Desjardins grinned at Atlas. "They hate buckwheat," she said. "Except Jada. You can have buckwheat pancakes anyway, Jaja."

"Yay!"

"Oh, man, I'm losing my marbles," said Mrs. Desjardins. "I didn't even ask where you live. What street are you on?"

"Vernon."

"Darn, I'm going the wrong way," she said, and rolling down her window to check for traffic, she did a one-handed U-turn that spun on the snow-hard surface and flung them all to the side. Atlas fumbled the Kritter Kube and it turned on, shrieking, "Feed me! Feed me!" and then leapt from his hands. He lunged, missed, and propelled it into the open ashtray where it dropped and disappeared.

"Feed me!"

"What the heck?" said Mrs. Desjardins.

"I'm sorry!"

"Kritter Kube!" shouted Jada, throwing her arms up into the air.

"Those are for babies," said Brodey with glee, "why've you got a baby toy?"

"Shut up, half-wit!" said Harper.

"Dip-wit!"

"Feed me!"

"That's it! Buckwheat pancakes!"

"Yay!"

This went on until they pulled up to Atlas' apartment building.

Atlas' face was burning. How could he do something so stupid in front of Harper? Again?

Mrs. Desjardins pulled out the ashtray and fished around, but the Kritter Kube had disappeared.

"Holy crap, it's gone down inside somewhere. I don't know how to get it out, but I guess—well, we'll figure it out at home."

"I'm sorry," said Atlas again. "It was an accident—I—"

"It's okay. Well, we've gotta get going, Atlas. We're a bit late now."

"I'm sorry!" he threw open the door and jumped out. "Thank you for the ride. And—" The car spun around and sped off. "—I'm really sorry!"

Why did he always have to act like such an idiot around Harper? And now in front of her whole family, too! He was just beginning to wonder how he'd show his face in school tomorrow when, from the corner of his eye, he saw Campbell heading up the street, encrusted in snow.

"Campbell!" he shouted, and the wind whipped he words away. He headed back down the street, but Campbell rushed up his driveway and into his house before he could catch up. Had Campbell seen him getting out of Harper's car? Did he know it was Harper's car?

Atlas held his stomach. He felt sick.

He turned back to his apartment building, not hearing the wind raging fiercely in his ears and not knowing whether the stinging in his eyes was pellets of snow or something from deep within.

CHAPTER TWENTY-FOUR

"Oh, good, you're home. Come in here, we've got something important to talk about!" His mother sounded excited.

Now what? Atlas hung up his parka and scarf and added his mittens and toque to the glove dryer sitting over the entryway heat register. Peter, his mom, Félix, and Uncle Liron—looking uncharacteristically subdued—were seated around the table.

"See my new glasses, Atlas?" said Peter, glowing with happiness. "Mom got an extra pair, too, so if these ones get broken, I can use *these*." He held up the case with the spare set.

"The new frames make him look like such a little man," said their mother.

Atlas looked again. He hadn't noticed new frames. "Yeah, they're nice—they're great." He couldn't tell any difference.

"Do you like them, Uncle Liron?" said Peter, turning. Uncle Liron shrugged.

"What's up with you?" said their mother.

Uncle Liron shrugged again, which made their mother narrow her eyes. He seemed to sense a losing battle and said, "I quit."

"Quit what?"

"Physiotherapy."

"What! Why? Liron! You're halfway through! You can't be serious."

"Yeah, I quit."

"But—I know you were struggling—it's not like you're not up to the work—what is it? We can sort it out."

"It's just not my thing."

"Liron!" Atlas heard the shock in his mother's voice. "Mamma's going to flip out—"

"I'll pay back the money. I'm lookin' for a job—"

"And you'd better hope you never run across Theodora or Sandrine, because they-will-*kill*-you!" These were the two oldest sisters in the family who, Atlas knew, were helping to finance Uncle Liron's way through university.

"Yeah, sure—but I'll be worse than dead if I stay on doing—"

"Liron! I can't believe my ears. Sitting there feeling sorry for yourself? And why? Because you have opportunities that half the world would give their right eye for—you do know that our parents—" Their mother was going into full-throttle shout, but Félix took her hand into his.

"Maybe . . . we give this some time and discuss a little later," he said, gently. Atlas was surprised to see his mother deflate and the anger drain from her face until she was looking at her youngest brother with only worry.

Peter said, "Is that the important thing you needed to talk to us about?

"No, sweetheart. No! It's—now that we're all here, I want to talk about Spain."

Atlas couldn't help it; he groaned.

"That's exactly why," she continued, putting her arm around his shoulder. "It was a nasty way to find out about it, by accident like that. I should have told you sooner, and I should have told you everything. I'm sorry."

"It's okay, mamma," said Peter.

"It's really not okay," she said, "but thank you for saying so. I'm going to try to make up for it. I know it won't be easy moving to another country, but at least I can give you the facts and equip you. The first fact is that my new job starts in the spring so that I have plenty of time to get ready before the fall term starts. And Félix's secondment here ends on April fifteenth. So that means we'll go to Valencia the following week."

"April! That's—that's really soon. School won't even be over!"

"Yes, I know, *Salta*. I guess I thought it would be easier for you and Peter if you didn't have to be expecting it for a long time."

"Like ripping a bandage," offered Félix.

"Yes, something like that. And that brings me to the second thing. We're all going together. You, Atlas, and Peter, and me, and Félix."

"What does that mean . . . *together*?" said Atlas.

"Are you and Félix getting married?" said Peter.

"No, Peter," said Félix, "but we want to be together. So, yes, we will become a family. I have an apartment in Valencia already, but it's tiny. We'll stay there until your mother and I can find a bigger, nicer place that's good for all of us."

"Will we live in an apartment again? Like now?" asked Peter.

"Yes, I think so," said their mother.

"Valencia is not like here," said Félix, "where people have such large houses so far apart from each other. Most people live in apartments."

"Good," said Peter. "I like apartments. Will it be big enough for Uncle Liron to come and stay? Will Uncle Liron come and visit?"

"I certainly hope so!" said their mother. They all looked at Uncle Liron and he shrugged noncommittally. Their mother said, "That's not okay," and she dived onto him and started tickling until he said, of course, of *course* he'd come.

Atlas didn't know what to say. Moving was one huge thing; but moving in with Félix—that was big. He looked down into his lap.

"The next thing is: I need to get you two started on learning Spanish. I've hired a tutor to come after school three times a week. It'll be a start, anyway, before we get there."

"Why can't *you* teach us? Or Félix?" said Peter.

"Sweetie, Félix and I already have full-time jobs. We wouldn't have time to be consistent enough."

"Anyway, I have no expertise at teaching languages to young children," said Félix.

"Who is it, then?"

"Her name is Mimi Abrantes, and you're going to love her. She'll come three times a week—working around your peewee schedule, Atlas, once you're back in hockey."

Atlas knew it was a good idea to start learning Spanish ahead of time, but he didn't know how he felt about being in a class of two with his younger, genius brother. "Peter'll be top of the class," said Atlas.

"I don't think so," his mother said. "You're already understanding Félix's and my conversations in Spanish, and you've had no instruction."

"Well, it's 'cause you talk in Spanish all the time," said Atlas.

"But not everyone can do that," said Félix, "—pick up a language that way. In fact, few people can."

"*I* can't," said Peter. "I've been listening to all the same stuff, and I don't know what they're saying."

"You have your mother's gift," said Félix.

"Yeah, you're just like Vita," said Uncle Liron.

"But—"

"It's a gift," said his mother, and kissed him on the forehead, looking very proud. He didn't know what to think.

"And there's one last thing."

What now?

His mother grinned and pulled up a bag from under the table. "In honour of Peter getting his new glasses, a bonus movie night! I got some videos on Spain from the library so we can all start learning together. We've got *A Short History of Spain*, *Spain Land of Sun and Spirit*, *Cooking with Señora Gongora*, *Spanish Castles*, *Spanish Stories and Myths*, and *Sports in Spain*. Where do you want to start?

"*Cooking with Señora Gongora*," said Liron—

"*Sports in Spain*," said Atlas—

"*Spanish Castles*," said Peter, all at the same time.

Their mother laughed. "Well, since this extra movie night is in honour of Peter, let's go with *Spanish Castles* to start with."

"Man, we're never gonna see *Cool Runnings*," said Uncle Liron.

"Patience little brother, patience."

So, after supper, they watched *Spanish Castles*. Against his predilection, Atlas was entranced. The castles were enormous and handsome, and each had its own character and there were so *many* of them; and their histories were cruel and bloody and astonishing. And he found that he enjoyed listening to the narrator speaking in Spanish, while comparing what he heard to the English subtitles. He could make out quite a bit already.

"Oh, look! He just said, *Yes, that's right*, but they didn't put that in the subtitles.

"Where?" said Peter.

"You're right," said his mother, "they often skip things in subtitles because people can't read as fast as they can listen, so it's hard to put every single thing in."

Atlas glanced over at Peter, who was watching intently, focused on the subtitles, and he realized his mom was right. He knew more Spanish than Peter did. How had that happened? Peter was more advanced than him in every subject. Had they stumbled upon something where he was smarter than Peter?

He wondered how Peter would do in school in Spain, and then he was stopped by another thought. If Peter had to struggle a little with the language, would that bring him a bit closer to the level of the other students in his grade? Would it make him more like the others? And would it, maybe, make it easier for him to make friends?

Atlas was so captivated by this strange question that he forgot to watch the castle show. Nor did he notice that he hadn't once that evening worried about his *own* transition into school in Spain but had been thinking only of Peter.

CHAPTER TWENTY-FIVE

Something unexpected was happening: Atlas continued to build the fort with Peter and Jimmy, but now a few other kids joined in. Not little kids from Peter's grade—those all got taken straight home by their parents. But some kids from the grades in between Atlas and Peter walked home on their own and sometimes hung around a bit, and a few of them came over to the fort. It made Atlas happy, because maybe Peter would be able to make friends with them. They weren't Peter's age, but closer to it than he or Jimmy. The new kids seemed wary of Jimmy at first, but Jimmy ignored everyone, so they all ignored him back, and soon there was a growing army of kids in snow pants compressing snow and pounding blocks onto the wall.

"The fort's getting huge!" said Peter.

"Yeah, it is," grinned Atlas. "More crooked, too, now that we've got all these helpers. They don't have a clue about building." It was hard to get the wall higher without things toppling over, so it had spread out, with three arms snaking in different directions. All the snow around the wall had been used and the naked ground was brown, with frozen grass poking up. Snow was being hauled from the back of the schoolyard.

"That's true," said Peter, "but I like it."

March had arrived and that meant Atlas' eight-game ban from peewees would soon be over and his team would be heading into their last few games of the season. Atlas had managed to hold his yearning for hockey in check by not letting it into his thoughts, but now it was *all* he could think about. Since there were other kids building the fort after school, he felt fine about leaving Peter until Félix could pick him up when he finished work.

The days were getting longer, and now the sun shone for hours after school was over, and the temperature was up and down so that some days were slushy. Parts of the wall were collapsing, but then a squall would blow in, covering the schoolyard in fresh snow, and repairs would be made.

It was Monday, it was sunny, he had survived his eight-game suspension from peewees and the embarrassment of hanging out on the junior side of the school with little kids and Jimmy Zimlinski, and Atlas was whistling. He was happy enough to almost—*almost* pretend the ache of missing Campbell wasn't there.

Then he heard, "Hey! You stepped right on my block."

"Yeah, I'll step on you if you don't get out of my way." Uh-oh, Jimmy Zimlinski was being ornery today.

"That's not fair!"

"You're a dork."

"Hey, stop pushing!"

"I'm gonna squish you, pinhead!"

Atlas rushed towards the end of the wall where the scuffle was going on, and he saw Jimmy lash out and all the other kids scatter—all except Peter, too-trusting Peter, who piped, "It's okay, Jimmy. It was a simple misunderstanding. It's okay."

Jimmy roared, swinging both arms, and caught Peter in the stomach. Peter went flying.

"Stop!" Atlas shouted. He knew that he was too skinny to make Jimmy stop, so he sped past Jimmy to Peter and pulled him away. "Come on!" He dragged Peter to his feet and rushed him to the entryway where their knapsacks were sitting. Jimmy didn't seem to be following.

"Are you okay?"

"Yeah," said Peter, but sounding a little shaky. "It didn't hurt too much with my parka on."

"Let's go home." Atlas swung on his knapsack and helped Peter get his on overtop his bulky parka, and he steered his little brother down the school driveway.

"What a nutcase," said Atlas.

"No he's not."

"Why do you stick up for him? That's the second time he attacked you for no reason."

"No, I think I was just in the wrong place at the wrong time. He didn't really hurt me this time. And look! My glasses aren't broken."

"That's not the point. He *could* hurt you next time he goes nuts. Why do you even like him?"

Peter considered for a moment. "I don't think I *like* him, exactly. But I like that he wants to help build the fort. And I just think he's . . ."

"He's what?"

Peter was silent, thinking, as if trying to find the right words.

"He's what?"

"You know the brain attic?"

"Yeah . . ."

"Well, that's for keeping ideas. But you need a heart house, too, where you keep things you love. And people. I think maybe his heart house is empty," said Peter.

"Do you—do you sit there filling up and organizing your heart house in class, too?" said Atlas, to this startling idea. "Like you do with your brain attic?"

"No, silly," said Peter, now laughing. "*Other* people have to fill it up!" and he ran ahead to jump in a little snow drift that the wind had sculpted across the sidewalk. Atlas shook his head. How could he understand this little brother of his? How could he keep him safe with thinking like this—so freakishly *different*. How was Peter ever going to make friends?

But one thing was clear. Peter trusted Jimmy Zimlinski far too much, and Atlas did not trust him at all. So, next morning, before the bell rang, Atlas went to see Mr. Wick.

"Coach," he said.

Mr. Wick frowned. "Mr. Wick, Atlas. You know that."

"Coach," said Atlas again, and perhaps a bit louder than he'd intended, for his throat felt as if it was seizing shut, "I don't think—I think—well, I've missed the last eight games and I'm out of practice and it wouldn't be fair to the team to come into playoffs like that. It would be a disadvantage to the team. So, I think I—I should stay off the team for the rest of the season."

"Atlas!" Mr. Wick had stood up very straight and was looking alarmed.

"That's what I think," said Atlas, and he turned and threw himself into his desk before Mr. Wick could respond. The other kids were coming in now, chattering, jostling, filling the room with noise and activity, and Atlas busied himself with getting out his binder and pencil case and pretended that Mr. Wick wasn't staring at him.

But at home that night, he poured out his jumbled thoughts and troubled feelings to Tim and even told him about the heart house.

"And I don't even know what Peter means about it and I don't know if I did the right thing and I quit hockey and it might be my last chance to play now that we're going to Spain, and I must be the stupidest person in the world!"

"Buddy, how can you say that? Just hold up there on calling yourself stupid."

"Maybe I should be like Jimmy Zimlinski and not care about anything!"

"Aww, buddy, you couldn't do it. You just wouldn't be able to."

"Why does it—why—just trying to figure out the right thing to do

—why does it have to be so *stupid*!" He pounded the stack of towels in the shelf.

"Why, that's what life is all about: making one decision, and then making another and another."

"That's bull—"

"You've been doing it all along. Everybody does. That's all we do, every day, all day long. A lot of people never think about why they decide one thing or another and they just get carried along by events. All of us do to some extent. But you—you're trying to make decisions *on purpose*. *For* a purpose. That means you're growing up. And I'll tell you what else. I don't know if I'd have been able to make the sacrifice you just did for your little brother. Why, I think you're already more of a man than I ever was."

Atlas didn't know what to say to this. "What're you talking about? You're a hero! To millions. You're *my* hero."

Tim smiled at him, but sadly. "Buddy, one thing you'll find out is whenever you make a person your hero, they're going to disappoint you."

"What d'you mean? What are you talking about, Tim?"

But he had faded away.

CHAPTER TWENTY-SIX

Atlas continued to feel angry, and he didn't even know why. His mother tried to talk him out of giving up hockey and eventually, when he explained why he'd done so, she said, "I'm sure the school will keep him safe."

He shocked himself by shouting at her: "Oh, yeah, like they did last time? That's easy for you to say, because you didn't have to watch him get beat up!" He was horrified, but somehow also fiercely satisfied by the look of dismay on his mother's face. *I'm sorry!* he wanted to say, *I wasn't strong enough to keep Peter safe from Jimmy Zimlinski. He's too big!* but he said, "Like you'd care," and stomped to his room.

When their mother said it was time to get the poor car clean because you couldn't even tell what colour it was anymore, Peter jumped up with both hands in the air crying, "Car wash!" and Atlas said, "That's baby stuff," and stomped off to his room. He heard them leave and lock the apartment door and wished he was with them.

When Mimi Abrantes—the Spanish tutor—came, he said, "I don't understand any of this," and Peter said, "Yes you do, Atlas! It's all there in your attic!" and Atlas said, "Attics are for bats and old junk," and stomped to his room.

At dinner, Peter complained that Atlas was locking him out of their room too much and it wasn't fair. Atlas said, "What's fair about having to share a room with a *baby*!"

Félix flared up, but his mother snorted.

"That's ridiculous, Atlas. Nobody's ever been less of a baby than Peter—even when he *was* a baby. I think you're just hav—"

"I'm not having puberty!" said Atlas fiercely; and to his surprise, his mother burst into giggles.

"Puberty? That's not what I was going to say. I was going to say I think you're just having a rough week. But now that you mention it: are you? Are you feeling a sudden growth spurt, or . . ."

"It's *not* funny!"

"So you *are*? Having a growth spurt?"

"I'm not growing—hair—or—"

Now everyone was laughing.

"He's growing horns!" said Peter.

"Hooves!"

"Warts?"

Atlas was conflicted between stomping off or staying and finishing his dinner, because he'd barely gotten started and he was starving. Lately, he was so hungry all the time. His mother leaned over and put her arm around him.

"*Salta*," she said; and he tried to shrug her arm away, but half-heartedly, "it's just teasing. I love you so, so much, and I know how sad you must be about giving up hockey."

"Yeah, Atlas," said Peter, "why'd you give it up? You should go back!" Atlas nearly ground his teeth. How could Peter be such a genius and yet not understand what was happening?

"You're so much like your dad," said his mother. "Not just in looks, and not just the kind eyes. The kind heart, too. And the sense of responsibility."

"Oh, yeah, responsibility, like going off to Toronto."

"Paving the way for us. We were going to join him, you remember."

Atlas was silent. He stared at his plate.

"Such a tragedy to be killed by that drunk driver," said Félix. Atlas clenched. He hated talking about this. He would normally have run from the room long before this point in the conversation. And why was Félix chipping in? He didn't even have his facts straight.

"You mean killed by that driver when he was wandering around drunk," said Atlas, angrily.

"What?" said his mother.

Vaguely, he registered her shock, but he continued. "Well, he shouldn't have gotten drunk and then walked home. He was probably weaving around in the middle of the road in the dark—" He stopped. His mother was staring at him.

"You think—you think—" tears welled up in her eyes. "You think *he* was drunk? The *driver* was drunk. Atlas, he was hit by a drunk driver. You know this. Why—you *know* this!"

Atlas looked at his mother in confusion. Her face was stricken. What was going on?

"How could I . . . You didn't? . . . Atlas, I thought you knew—you didn't understand this?" and she clasped him tight, so tight, in a desperate clench and then she let him go and covered her face with her hands and her shoulders shook in sobs.

Atlas looked around at the others. Peter's face was all big eyes and a little O mouth, and Félix was looking from one to the other in confusion.

"Mom," Atlas whispered, afraid. His heart was thumping horribly. "Mom, Mom—he wasn't drunk?"

She shook her head.

"But I thought . . . I—I" Atlas didn't know what he thought. His brain didn't seem to be working and his chest had frozen and now his throat was frozen and he couldn't speak. He stood up, and his cutlery clattered down onto his chair. He was no longer hungry, not the least little bit; and he went to his room and shut the door.

❖

He became aware that there was quiet knocking, maybe there had been for some time now.

"Atlas, let me in." It was Peter. Oh. Okay. He got up and unlocked the door. Peter came in, and Atlas walked out. He went to the bathroom.

"Buddy, I've been waiting for you."

"Do you know what happened?"

Tim nodded.

"How could I—Tim, how could I have got that mixed up? How—I thought that's what they said! All this time, I thought he was a drunk and got himself killed and I've been *hating* him—*hating* him! How—I —" and then he couldn't talk anymore. Distantly in his memory, like looking down a long, dark lane—how could it have become so distant, this memory that was burned into his soul? He saw his mother walking into their room. He was sitting on his bed amidst a mountain of toy building pieces and wooden train track sections. Peter was sleeping on the other side of the room, his auburn hair curled with sweat, his chubby little hand pressed up under his cheek. The afternoon sun streamed in.

She sat on the bed next to him and he remembered the weight of her as she sat down and how his toys all tumbled towards her. Her face looked so odd, with an expression he didn't know, and she said, "Atlas, I have to tell you something really important. It's going to be very hard to understand."

"What is it?"

"Your dad—" she stopped; started again. "Daddy's not coming back. He—"

"Why? Why's he not coming back? For how long?"

"No, sweetheart. He's not—he—Atlas, he was killed. Daddy's . . ."

"Killed?"

"Yes. Oh, I'm so sorry, sweetheart!"

"What do you mean killed? Killed like he's—dead?"

"Yes, Atlas, he was killed. Oh, Atlas, Daddy's not homing home!" And she hugged him, the way she had tonight. So tight, so desperate.

The memory of it was suffocating. He hadn't thought about that moment for a long time, and now he couldn't stop crying.

CHAPTER TWENTY-SEVEN

"I don't feel well," said Atlas. "I don't think I can go to school today."

He knew he didn't fool his mother. He wasn't sick, not in the way you were supposed to be to miss school; but he'd never felt so sick in his life. How could he ever repair the damage to the memory of someone he loved so much, and whom he'd spent the last three years hating, and who was dead and gone so that he could never express his remorse?

His mother looked so searchingly into his face that he had to look away.

"Okay," she said at last, "I'll call in sick. Lucky thing it's Friday. That'll give us time to get you better for school on Monday, so I'll only have to miss one day." He recognized the message. She understood his need for solitude right now, but she couldn't afford to take another day off work; he would have to go back to school on Monday, even if he didn't feel any happier then. And he couldn't imagine how he would. He would never be happier.

Atlas nodded, not looking at her. Would she get in trouble for staying home when she wasn't really sick? But he couldn't—

"I can stay on my own," he offered. "It's legal, 'cause I'm eleven."

"It's legal," said his mother, smoothing his bristly hair, which was sticking up in spikes all over, as if he'd been writhing in his bed all night, "but it wouldn't be good. I can use a day off anyway. Time to catch up on laundry and books. Do you want to lie on the couch and read?"

Atlas shook his head.

But he didn't know what to do with himself. The things he'd usually have loved—reading comics, working through his Big Book of Word Puzzles, poring over last year's Ice Hockey Annual—all seemed meaningless. He sat and stared out the window into the apartment courtyard at the frozen little kids' playground and the endless snow eddies blown up by the tempestuous wind. After a while, he couldn't stand being in his room anymore. He wandered out and found his mother in her room, tucked up with a novel and a mug of tea.

"Mom, can I watch TV?"

She looked up from her book. "No, *Salta*," she said. "Daytime TV will rot your brain. But you can watch movies from the kids' shelf—whatever you want."

"Thanks, Mom."

He trolled through the shelf and dragged off *The Future is Wild.* There were enough episodes for him to watch for a long time, and the subject of where evolution might take the planet in five, ten, or twenty-million years' time was fantastical and remote enough to carry him away—away from his troubles. He'd seen the videos before. He watched without really paying much attention, and all the time his mind was running frantically on another track; but quiet enough that there were minutes at a time when he didn't feel nauseous with self-loathing.

Some time later, he felt a presence at his side, and his mother was there. She set down a bowl of leftover beef barley soup, a grilled cheese sandwich, and a glass of milk on the coffee table.

"Think you can manage this?" she said.

Atlas nodded. She sat on the couch beside him. A question had been boiling inside him, one that he hadn't meant to voice, but it burst out.

"Mom, why didn't he—didn't he—why'd he have to go to Toronto? Why didn't he love us enough to stay here?"

"Oh, Atlas! He loved us enough, oh, he loved you so much!"

"But he went!"

"He wanted to stay."

"Then why didn't he?"

"It was me, Sweetheart. I insisted he go."

Atlas whipped around and stared at his mother. "But *why*? Why would you *do* that? Didn't you love him?"

"I loved him, I loved him so much. That's why I did it."

Atlas yelped in a kind of outrage, but she quelled him gently. "This is hard to understand. Your dad loved music so much, and when it came to reggae . . . Well, for him it was like . . . He just drank it in, swam in it. When he was playing with his band, he came alive—totally alive."

"But—!"

"But he loved us more. Being a musician isn't one of those things that society often rewards. We all love music, we want to be entertained, soothed, sung to, made happy or accompanied in our bereavement; but we don't want to pay for it in the same way that we're happy to pay for roads or schools or . . . Well, anyway, your dad struggled. We were barely making a living, and he blamed himself, and you boys were growing up. He gave up music and took a job in a restaurant and we were getting along, but it made me sad. He was cheerful, he spent all his free time with you boys, but I could see that it was making him smaller and smaller. You see, Atlas, it's not just that he loved music—he was talented, truly talented at it. It was what his soul was made of, the gift he had to give the world. So, when he stopped . . ."

"You mean—like Tim Horton with hockey?"

"Yes, maybe something like that. Born to it. Everybody has a gift, something only they can give, and that was his."

"I don't have a gift," mumbled Atlas.

"You do," said his mother gently, "you just haven't found it yet. Some people find it early and some later, but whatever it is . . . Well, if a person can't give their gift, it's a kind of imprisonment."

"Like being punished?"

"It can certainly feel like that, but it's more than a punishment, because it feels as if you can never get out. A life sentence."

Atlas thought about this for a while. In one way, it made sense. He could imagine Tim Horton feeling like a prisoner if he'd been told he couldn't play hockey anymore. But Atlas' heart was twisting fretfully this way and that, pounding out: *No, no, he had to love us more!*

His mother continued. "So, when your dad's bandmates came and said they'd landed a string of gigs in Toronto and would he go?—he said *no*, but I insisted. The reggae scene is a lot bigger there than it is here, so the scope was great, the chances of them being able to make it so much better. The first three months were a terrible struggle, and then they started getting some regular gigs and they started being known. Your dad was saving money and he was just about ready to put down first and last month's rent on an apartment, and then we were to all go—"

"I didn't know that!" said Atlas. "I always thought he was supposed to come back here."

"We didn't want to tell you until we were sure. We were just starting to work out the plans—who would drive with me all the way to Ontario, hauling our stuff—because he was so busy with gigs that he couldn't fly back. And then . . . Well, then there was nothing to be done."

"So, he really wanted to be with us?"

"Yes, he really did."

Atlas remembered something Tim had told him. "One time Tim said, 'In any family, there are puzzles that can't be solved,'" he said. "Was it like that?"

"Who's Tim?"

"Tim Horton!"

"Oh. I didn't know he said that. Well, it's true."

"Yeah . . . And why—how—how did it happen?" Atlas' voice seemed to strangle in his throat, but he pressed on and said, barely in a whisper. "The drunk driver."

She told him everything.

Then, after a long time he said, "Did you tell me all this before? I mean when . . . ?"

"Yes, Sweetheart."

"But why did I think *he* was drunk?"

"I don't know, *Salta*."

"Did you tell me *everything*? Everything you just told me now?" he said, desperately, pleading with his eyes.

"Yes, everything."

"Then how could I—how *could* I—?" and he burst into tears and didn't even care that he was blubbering in front of this mother, with tears obliterating his vision and his nose running; and his mother sat close, one arm tight around him, and let him cry.

CHAPTER TWENTY-EIGHT

Days passed. Atlas walked to school with Peter, sat in his desk, did his assignments, ate lunch alone, went back to class, built the shrinking slush fort with Peter and Jimmy Zimlinski and the others, and walked back home with Peter. His body was heavy, his heart had gone dark, his voice had abandoned him. Peter looked apprehensive, and he didn't know how to help that. Peter, normally quiet, became even more so, which made Atlas worry, and that made him feel even heavier.

"Has there been a vow of silence I didn't know about?" said his mother at dinner, trying to lighten the mood.

"What's a vow of silence?" said Peter, and their mother explained about monks and Félix gave some Spanish examples, and Peter began to quiz them about it and said that he needed to know so much more to prepare for Spain. He made notes about books he would have to search for in the library, and Atlas was thankful that the attention had been steered away from him. But he saw his mother cast an anxious look his way.

Campbell continued to avoid him at school, but Atlas had stopped trying to catch his eye. There didn't seem to be any point. He didn't know how to change things.

And now Tim wasn't showing up. Why now? Why, when more than ever he needed help—when he needed someone who knew what to do? Once again, he went through his mental catalogue of men he knew: Campbell's dad?—as if. Félix?—no way! Coach?—well, that was impossible now, and even as Coach, Atlas didn't think Mr. Wick was up to understanding what was going on, much less what might be needed. Finally, reluctantly, he decided to talk to Uncle Liron.

But the next time Uncle Liron came over, he sat on the couch and stared and couldn't be enticed into conversation or even a game of Jenga.

"What's going on?" their mother asked. "Did you . . . Have you . . ." Atlas could see she was grasping. Uncle Liron had already dropped out of university and they'd already gone through the pains of him finding a new job; so what could it be now? "Did you break up with your . . . girlfriend?"

"I don't have a girlfriend," said Liron, sounding angry.

"Then . . . ?"

"I don't want to talk about it."

"Okay . . ."

Peter jumped onto the couch next to him. "I read something!" he piped. "It was a new term that I didn't know, and even after I looked it up I didn't understand what it was about, so I had to do some research. Is it unrequited love? That's when you love somebody and they—"

But Atlas didn't hear the rest, because to his amazement, tears welled up in Uncle Liron's eyes and their mother said, "Shht, Peter, we know what unrequited love is," and Uncle Liron got up and went to the bathroom, and Peter fell silent. Atlas wasn't sure *he* knew what unrequited love was, but he was embarrassed to ask. When Uncle Liron finally emerged from the bathroom, he said he couldn't stay for dinner after all and left, and their mother looked sober.

So, it was obvious that Uncle Liron would be no help.

At school, things were no better, down to Mr. Wick shouting

"Crickets!" which he couldn't seem to help himself doing at least once a day. This made everyone laugh, which, to the class' delight, infuriated him further. But Atlas didn't laugh. He was wistful for Coach. He almost couldn't remember how fun and supportive Coach could be, and now he only saw Mr. Wick—and a Mr. Wick who, recently, was much touchier than usual. The others might laugh, but Atlas only felt humiliation at being reminded every day how dismally he had failed at Valentine's Day and at winning over Harper.

But that wasn't entirely true. For reasons he didn't understand, Harper had been friendlier to him than *before* the horrible Valentine's Day party. Indeed, her friendliness and them laughing together was what had caused the rift with Campbell. Atlas didn't understand that either. He noticed Campbell's many twitches, in a way that he'd never seen before, but so what? Campbell was no different now than he had been since becoming Atlas' best friend at the very start of grade one.

Atlas was supposed to be writing a book report, but instead he drew a big black cloud in his book and under it he wrote a list of things he didn't understand:

1. How girls think.
2. How to ixplain mistakes.
3. How to not be embarasing.
4. ~~How to tell Campbell he is the best. Why won't Campbell at least~~ How can I ixplain what happened?
5. How to help Peter.
6. What to do in Spain with no hockey.
7. ~~How could Mom~~ ~~Why did Mom~~ I dont understand.
8. How could I of made such a big mistake?

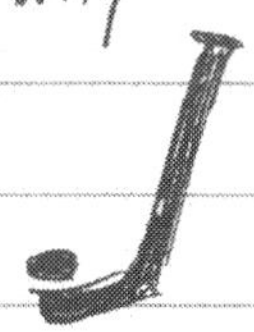

Atlas stared at the page. Writing things down didn't help, it only made everything worse. There it all was, staring him back in the face, and he didn't know how to answer *any* of those questions.

Mr. Wick approached from behind, clearing his throat. Atlas quickly turned the page and wrote: Trapped in Ice, by Eric Walters.

"You'd better get going, Atlas," said Mr. Wick behind him. "You're running out of time."

"Yeah."

And then he didn't speak again for most of the rest of the day.

At lunch, he overheard fragments of conversation between Harper and her friends a couple of tables over.

"Do you think I could write him a note?"

"I don't know . . ."

"I just want to explain . . ."

"It wasn't . . ."

"But it hurt his feel . . ."

Atlas supposed they must be talking about Campbell, and he found that it did make him feel a little bit better to know that Harper was sorry for the trouble she'd caused.

After school, he lay on his bed watching Peter read and draw in his notebook. Scenes played in his head of Spanish kids jeering and pushing Peter around. In his imagination, they were dark and muscular and brimming with confidence, like the bullfighters in the documentaries. Atlas was filled with trepidation for Peter—for both of them—going to school in Spain.

Peter must have felt Atlas' gaze, and he looked up; and as if they'd been discussing it all along, he said, "What does Tim say to do?"

"Tim? Well . . . not much. But—yeah, I'm gonna go ask him." It was worth a try. If Tim appeared, he was going to start by demanding to know why he wasn't showing up all the time, especially when Atlas needed him so much. But he forgot all about that when Tim *was* there.

"Hey, buddy," said Tim, and Atlas was relieved to see that Tim's eyes were crinkled up smiling and not filled with concern like the other adults around him.

"Tim, how do I—how—well, I don't know what the right question is," said Atlas.

"Just tell it to me from the top," said Tim.

So, Atlas did. When he got to the end, he said, "How can I, I don't know, change or—"

"Make it all better," supplied Tim.

"Yeah, how can I fix it?"

"Well, you can't. That much I *did* learn."

"But—"

"You can't change it, so you can never fix it, exactly. But you can change the way you go on ahead. From now on. I think you're already starting to do that, and it's all anyone ever can do."

"But how's the best way?"

"Only you can answer that."

"But I don't have *any* answers!"

"Most of us don't, buddy, most of us don't."

Atlas sighed, and his shoulders sagged. "But, this isn't—this isn't helping! I don't know *anything*, and if you don't either . . ."

"Now, I didn't say that. There's one thing here that I know for certain, and I think you do, too, and that's that your dad was a real hero."

"Yeah," said Atlas slowly, "I guess he was. But, Tim, he's dead. I can't ask him anything. He can't help me! I don't know if he would—he never did before, so I guess—no one else will come to me in the mirror like you. I guess . . . Well, at least you can. You're my hero."

Now it was Tim who sighed, but much heavier than Atlas; it was almost a groan. He looked down for a long moment, as if he were gazing at his invisible feet, somewhere beyond the mirror; and then he met Atlas square in the eye. "Your dad's much more of a hero than I ever was. *Much* more. He tried to put his family first, even if it didn't work out, and me—why, I was killed because of my own stupidity. I'd been drinking—a lot—before I got in that car and headed down the highway. I was driving drunk. Luckily, I didn't hurt any . . ."

Atlas didn't hear the rest. His ears were ringing. His heart was surging with fear and disbelief and a feeling of crumbling, and he stared into the mirror. Just stared and stared without saying or hearing anything. After a while, he saw that Tim's face settled into a sad, small grin—a crooked smile so tiny in that long, strong jaw.

And Atlas stared; and Tim faded away.

CHAPTER TWENTY-NINE

Atlas got a job delivering the community paper after school.

"I thought newspapers had to be delivered early in the morning so people can read them with their coffee while taking breakfast," said Félix.

"This is the local neighbourhood paper," explained their mother. "It's more about community events than news, so people don't care about having it hot off the press in the morning."

"How curious," said Félix. "May I see?" Atlas handed him a copy. It was half the dimensions of a normal newspaper, more like an oversized magazine, and featured articles about upcoming dances and fundraisers, awards won by locals, and lost and found pets—as well as the crossword puzzle, the word search, the codeword puzzle, and the weekly jokes submitted by kids. Félix seemed to find it highly entertaining.

The papers were left in tight bundles in the apartment building foyer during the day for Atlas to pick up and deliver later. So now, as soon as Atlas walked Peter home, he wrestled his mom's grocery trolley down the stairs, packed in the newspapers, and headed out again. Peter had to come, too, since there was no adult home until later, and this slowed things up considerably. But Atlas didn't mind. Peter loved it, and it seemed like a healthy thing getting him away from his books for a while. And it meant that by the time they were finished the rounds, it was suppertime. School, paper delivery, supper, homework, and bed, with no time in between; no time for his thoughts to bother him. He had a notion that getting a paying job was doing something his dad would approve of, and if he was looking down from heaven, he'd be proud. Atlas was earning money that he could contribute to . . . He wasn't sure what. His mom wouldn't have to buy him hockey equipment in Spain, sadly; but surely there would be something else—something else he could help with.

And lurking behind these thoughts was a vague idea, one he didn't allow to surface at all, of having enough money to take Harper to a Junior game before the season was over; before he went to Spain and never saw her again . . .

He was aware, sometimes, of snatches of quiet conversations between his mom and Félix:

"Well, at least he's keeping himself busy."

"But he's still so sad."

"Time heals, *amor*."

—and such things. He ignored it. He knew his mom was worried, and he didn't want to worry her, but he didn't know how to make himself happy. Whatever Tim had said, he didn't know what to do about *anything*. And Tim . . . He couldn't think about that. He hated—he couldn't—Better not . . . Better to keep busy.

One evening he heard something that sounded more urgent: "I just don't think that would be wise," said his mother.

"No, no," countered Félix, "Then he would see! It would lessen his sense of self-blame."

"But it could really go the other way."

"I think it would help."

"It would be so painful!"

"No more than the current pain—and it's more true."

He supposed they must be talking about him, but about what, specifically, he had no clue. Like so many adult conversations.

At school the next day before the first bell rang, Harper rushed up behind him and said, "Can-you-give-this-to-Campbell-for-me-please?-please-'cause-I'm-a-bit-scared," and she pressed a note into his hand and hurried off.

He stared at the paper. It had been folded many times until it was tiny and then taped shut. *Campbell* was printed in small, careful letters on each side. He turned it over. Campbell. This is what he should be doing. Maybe it was a way to get him to listen even if Campbell wouldn't allow him to speak directly. So, all during the morning, he snatched whatever moments he could, without being caught by teachers, to craft an apology letter. He wished he had Peter's gift for using drawings to illustrate ideas. That seemed like it would be a more effective way of getting across his deep feelings of remorse and sadness and loneliness, feelings which he couldn't even name. But all he had was words. And all the while, Harper's note sat in his pocket, with an extraordinary weight, and he was aware of her, across the aisle, biting her nails.

He wrote:

Dear Campbell. I don't know how to ixplain to you so you will understand, but I will try because I really miss you and your my best ~~firend~~ ~~freind~~ friend. I never wanted anybody else to be my best friend and I still don't. I just feel pretty terrible with you not talking to me. I know it seemed like we were making fun of you that day in the lunch room, but we werene't we were laughing about everybody. My mom says everybody has there funny ways. That's what we were laughing about. But your funny ways are what make you way better than any best friend I know about. ~~Tim says~~ Adults say you shouldn't have heros because they will always disappoint you. But you are better than a hero.

Atlas

At lunchtime, once again, Atlas had to search for Campbell; but this time, he was in the lunchroom, sitting with Gavin Eccles and Luis Lamenca. Gavin and Luis were pushing each other and laughing, but Campbell was mostly quiet. He looked very big next to the others, and Atlas wondered if this was how he and Campbell looked together. He was so skinny, and Campbell was muscular and tall and, since making mud pies in kindergarten, Campbell had always done everything better —or so it seemed to Atlas. How could he ever think that he, Atlas, would look down on him?

He marched over to Campbell and, before he had a chance to do more than look up and register that Atlas was in front of him, he shoved the note into Campbell's hand.

"Read it please," said Atlas. "Just read it!" He turned and walked away fast, so that Campbell couldn't protest or throw the note back at him. Then he went over to where Harper was sitting with Kelsey and Tiny. He handed her back the note she had given him that morning.

"I'm sorry," he said, "I just—"

Harper's shoulders sagged. "I knew you were going to say that."

"It just doesn't seem right," said Atlas. "For it to come from me, I mean."

"Yeah, I know . . ."

"I'm sorry," said Atlas, and then he left the lunchroom feeling strange, confused, afraid, but somehow also proud. He couldn't make sense of it at all.

After school, Atlas went to get Peter. The snow fort was melting fast now, so there was no point building it anymore, and everyone was now busy pulping it into rivers of slush and flinging slimy balls at each other.

"Come on, Peter!"

They walked home and then out again to do paper deliveries in the bright sunlight, unzipping their parkas and pulling off their toques. They stuffed their scarves down into the trolley under the newspapers.

The cart was much harder to pull through slush than over frozen snow. Atlas pulled, reaching down to free the wheels of slush at every stop, while Peter dipped in, grabbed a paper, and ran them up the sidewalks to doorsteps and mailboxes. It was now quite useful to have Peter along.

By the time they got to Campbell's house, the cart was nearly empty, because this was one of the last stops. Campbell was standing on the doorstep. Atlas' heart jumped up a couple of notches and then seemed to stop. Peter ran to the doorstep.

"Hi, Campbell!" he said, holding out a newspaper. Campbell took it and set it down on the doorstep and then he came down and walked home with them. Still silent, but walking with them.

CHAPTER THIRTY

At the lobby, as usual, they stopped to get the mail before heading upstairs. Atlas let Peter do it, because he loved the tiny key and the little door and stretching up to get the letters. Today, though, stretch as he would, he couldn't get the mail out.

"It's stuck, Atlas. There's something in there that's too big."

Atlas could see that the mail was well jammed. He wrestled the wad free, and in the middle was a package in a bubble-wrap envelope, torn at the edge where it had caught in the hinges. Atlas flipped it over and read:

To: Atlas Raphael

What? He never got mail. And especially not packages! He hadn't sent away for something long ago that he'd forgotten about, had he? Well, that was silly; he sent away for things so seldom that he'd never have forgotten. He searched for the return address, and that was even weirder:

Félix Fabiano Maior de Ruiz
Department of Linguistics

Craigie Hall
University of Calgary Main Campus
2940 University Way, N.W.,
Calgary, AB, T2N 1N4

Félix? Why was Félix sending him mail? Was he in trouble? What had happened? He showed Peter, and they pelted upstairs.

Inside, he tore open the package. A videotape burst out and fell onto the floor, followed by a single, thin page, which fluttered down and settled on top. Atlas picked up the paper.

Atlas—it said,

Before putting this video into the player, ask for some privacy from your little brother. You should see this on your own. It may be hard to watch, but it's very important. The most important thing, actually, is to listen. Give it at least five minutes and then open the letter inside the package.

Félix

P.S. Sorry it's in this format. It was never put onto DVD.

What . . . ? Atlas dug inside and pulled out an envelope. He held it in one hand and the tape in the other, feeling stupid.

"What is it?" said Peter.

Atlas handed him the note, and Peter read it.

"I wonder what it is!" said Peter. "Do you think after you watch it you'll be able to let me see, too?"

"I don't know," said Atlas.

"Well, it's okay," said Peter; but Atlas could see he was disappointed. "I have lots to do in our room. Will you tell me when I can come out?"

Atlas nodded. He went over to the old video player, mostly abandoned, at the very bottom of the big living room bookshelf; but it was still hooked up to the TV. He turned everything on and slid in the video.

There were some jumpy cuts where someone had done some inexpert editing and then a scene came into focus.

People were milling around a room. It looked like somebody's living room. They were dressed up in suits and dresses, and there were trays of sandwiches on tables. People were sitting in small groups or else standing and talking, and some little kids were rushing around, but they were shushed and told not to make noise. The camera panned around and with a lurch, Atlas saw that he was looking at himself, but much younger. He was so skinny and small. He was sitting in a big armchair and Peter, chubby and practically a baby, was nestled into his side, almost sleeping. Atlas' arm was around Peter, and his eyes were roaming, roaming, roaming around the room as if they were hunting. His face wore a strange expression. And he knew where he was. It was after his dad's funeral. He didn't know whose house it was, but he remembered this. He had tried not to: he had successfully forgotten it until now. Why would Félix want to show him this? How *could* he?

Atlas was about to yank the video out of the player, and he thought about throwing it off the balcony as far as he could hurl it. But the note had said *The most important thing is to listen.* What did that mean? Curiosity and a strange fascination kept him rooted.

But there was nothing to listen to. The camera had panned away from him and Peter, and there was a quiet buzz of subdued conversation, indistinct. But then a word jumped out of the jumble: *Rory*. His dad's name. More buzzing. *So terrible . . . Drunk*. Buzzing. *DVan*. His dad's reggae name. *Boys . . .* He heard his own name, and then, again, the word *drunk*.

The camera came back to him and his brother, looking lost in that big chair. Their mother approached. He got up and pulled Peter up, floppily, then she sat down, and Atlas climbed into her lap and she pulled up Peter, who nodded off again, and the three of them sat there together. Alone.

Atlas turned off the video. He wiped tears from his cheeks—still feeling angry at Félix, but mostly awash in deep sadness. He looked at the letter in his lap. Well, what could Félix want to say to him after that?

Dear Atlas,

I am sorry to bring you back to such a sorrowful day, but it's important for you to understand. Your mother showed me this video months ago, to help me understand you boys—and her. And from the moment of watching it, I understood that I am fortunate to be with a family that has great love.

You are punishing yourself for having carried the false belief that your father was drunk when, in fact, it was the driver who hit him who was drunk. How could such a false belief have happened?

But look at this small boy that you were, Atlas. In such a situation, nobody thinks clearly, much less an eight-year-old who has just lost his beloved father. And what was everyone talking about all around you—but not clearly, in hushed secret voices: drunk, drunk, drunk. Is it any wonder that this is the word that stuck in your head? Is it any wonder that a small, grieving boy could get confused and think that "drunk" meant your father? And if that was what that small, grieving boy believed, how could you blame him for being too heartsick to ever talk about it? And since he never talked about it, how could the mistake have been made right? And if the mistake was not made right until now, Atlas, that is not something for which to blame yourself.

You have never dishonoured your father, Atlas, for anyone can see that you loved him more than all the world; and you still do.

Félix

Atlas stared at the letter for a long time, reading it over and over. Was this what had happened? It seemed so. He had never seen this video before, and even if he had, he didn't think he would have picked up the confusing conversation if Félix hadn't pointed it out to him.

But now he knew the real story. He had already learned that he didn't have to hate his father any longer, and now, perhaps, he didn't need to despise himself. He let out a long sigh, and he stretched out along the length of the couch, the letter in his hand, and went to sleep.

CHAPTER THIRTY-ONE

"Can Campbell come and visit us in Spain?"

"That'll be up to his parents."

"But if his parents say he can—"

"Of course! Though we have no way of knowing if they would. But I can promise you this: we'll be coming back here to Calgary every once in a while."

"We will?!"

"Yes, we definitely will."

"Yay!" shouted Atlas, and he got up and ran around the table with his arms in a victory salute. Peter clattered out of his chair and ran after Atlas, shouting, "Hooray!"

"And, since you seem to be finished with breakfast, out the door!" said their mother sternly; but she was smiling, too.

Suddenly, they really were moving to Spain. Boxes were packed and furniture was sold. The apartment was emptying. Atlas and Peter had been asked to choose one box each of favourite books and toys and the rest would be given away—one box! Atlas put his comic books and hockey cards flat in the bottom and stacked his hockey books on top of them. After that, the decisions became harder.

"That includes the DVDs you want!" called their mother.

"DVDs! Don't we have a separate box for them?"

"'Fraid not."

"But there's not enough space!"

"I'm sorry, but it won't make sense to bring most of our things all the way to Spain. Shipping costs a lot, and it'll be cheaper to buy things there."

So, *Secondhand Lions* went into the box. He and Peter debated for a long time about *The Future is Wild* because it was a box set, so it took up the space of three other DVDs. In the end, they were so undecided that they tossed dice. *The Future is Wild* went in. But when it came to *Tim Horton—Heroes of Hockey*, Atlas sat on his bed, holding it in his hands and staring at it. A short time ago, this would have been one of the first things he put in the box. His memories of watching it were wrapped in happiness, and he wanted that happiness to stay with him; but now, Tim . . . Now he tried not to think about Tim, because it was too complicated. He was furious with him for driving drunk. Tim had killed himself for no reason! And deep down, where Atlas didn't even admit it to himself, he ached with sadness and grief at the loss of the simple, wonderful belief he had had in his hero. And he was confused. How could he—and the whole world—believe one thing about Tim and find out it was so wrong? Maybe he had misunderstood. Maybe he had made a terrible mistake.

But Tim had not come again, so he couldn't ask him.

Atlas and Campbell were spending every possible minute together, not daring to talk about leaving day. And Harper continued to gnaw at Atlas. He couldn't ask her to walk home together anymore because Peter was always with him; he should have done it earlier. And all the hockey league playoffs were over, except for the real playoffs: the Stanley Cup. The Flames were battling with the Canucks in the Conference Quarter Final, Calgary against Vancouver. Everyone was sure this was the year for the Flames, and the whole city was in Flames fever! Wouldn't it be amazing to go with Harper to a playoff game? But, of course, he didn't have *nearly* enough money for a ticket, even with everything he'd saved from delivering papers, and the tickets were all sold out anyway.

He daydreamed about watching games on TV with Harper, but he was too scared to invite her over to the apartment.

And anyway, they'd have left Canada before the end of even the Quarter Finals. Atlas had badgered Félix about watching the playoffs from Spain, and Félix had promised he'd find out how; but his mom said, "You'll be watching the games taped because hockey time here will be in the middle of the night there." Then she and Peter had gotten into a long discussion about time zones and daylight savings time and how time zones had been decided and the discovery of longitude, how it had transformed ocean travel and exploration and global connectedness generally, and that even though Easter Island was in the same time zone as them it was summer there now because it was in the southern hemisphere, and that was the difference between longitude and latitude, and so on.

Atlas went back to packing.

Morning walks to school now were in bright sunshine, and he and Peter would head first to Campbell's house. Today, Campbell wasn't quite ready, so they had to wait a minute, then the three of them walked on. As they stopped at the lights at the corner, a car pulled alongside and Atlas heard, faintly, "Feed me! Quick!" and then a woman's voice screamed, "When is that vile thing's battery *ever* going to die?"

In horror, Atlas ducked to Campbell's other side to hide. Harper's car! Was he never going to stop being embarrassed in front of her? The car pulled away, and Campbell and Peter seemed not to have noticed anything.

Atlas sighed. He didn't know what to do about Harper. He thought about asking Tim for advice, and then he remembered about Tim and he had to tramp down his feelings because their turbulence made him feel nearly as dizzy as standing atop a great height. He went back to worrying about Harper, and that gave him vertigo, too. So, he held onto the new feeling he had, the fierce feeling of loving his father again; but as wonderful as that was, it was too intense. So he tried to just pay attention to Campbell and Peter talking about the playoffs, but that reminded him that he would soon be leaving Campbell behind; and *that* reminded him how nervous he was about Spain and made him worry about how he would help Peter make friends there . . .

It seemed, these days, that he was awash in nothing *but* feelings.

At school, Mr. Wick organized a surprise goodbye party, which amazed Atlas, because Mr. Wick had never seemed to stop being angry with him since the Valentine's Day party. But Mr. Wick smiled and said kind things, and everybody gave Atlas a card they had made. When Harper gave him hers, her arm brushed his and made his whole body prickle. She leaned in close and whispered, "I put my address inside, Atlas. Will you write to me from Spain?"

Write? What? Actual letters? "Y—yes. Yes!"

Harper grinned, the little scar on her lip making her smile just a tiny bit, most charmingly lopsided. Atlas' head spun, and he immediately started worrying about learning to write letters properly.

❖

And then, he and Peter were in the back seat of the car with Uncle Liron sitting on Peter's other side, jiggling his leg up and down so ferociously that he jostled the whole seat in double-time, and Félix, in the front, was checking a long list, and their mother laughed as she took the turn off to the airport and said, "It's too late now! Anything that got forgotten is in the past. We're on a new adventure!"

Atlas wondered if he would ever be that happy about moving to Spain, and he once again remembered what Tim had told him: *In any family, there are puzzles that can't be solved.* Well, that was true, and in spite of everything, Tim had given him some good advice. Inwardly, he sighed deeply.

At the airport, they said goodbye to Uncle Liron in the parking lot. He said he couldn't bear to come into the airport to watch them disappear. He said gaining a car was hardly compensation for losing a family, but they could tell he was still happy about getting the wheels. He walked them to the parking lot entrance. They all hugged him, and their mother smoothed down his hair.

"You're letting it get long and messy," she said.

"Nah, I'm growing it out. I'm gonna have dreads."

"Dreads! Following in DVan's footsteps?"

"No, trying to make my own footsteps."

Their mother looked him searchingly in the eyes and said, "Don't get lost, Liron, don't get lost. And stay in close touch."

He assured them that he wouldn't get lost—*Whatever that means*, thought Atlas—but as he walked back towards the car, Atlas thought that Uncle Liron looked very alone.

Once they had checked in their bags and gone through security, there was a lot of time before their flight, so they walked around the airport.

"Tim Hortons!" cried Peter, pointing.

"Yes, let's," said their mother, dragging them forward. "One last time before we leave." Félix grumbled and said how he couldn't wait for a proper *café con leche* at his favourite coffee shop, and their mother jabbed him in the ribs with her elbow, "You wait," she said, laughing. "Within a month, you'll be pining for snow and whining for a Tim's."

Peter ran to a booth and clambered into the seat; Félix and their mother sat opposite him.

"I just—I have to go to the washroom," said Atlas, and he rushed off. He had to see . . . just one last time. It was a one-cubicle bathroom, so he locked the door behind him. No one else could come in. Feeling bitter, disconsolate, hopeful, and afraid all at the same time, he stepped up to the mirror.

Atlas. It was only his face.

He stood there for a long time, waiting, but Tim didn't appear.

He sighed. He wasn't sure how he felt. And he remembered what Tim had said to him: *I really don't think you even need me*. Maybe he was right.

When he got back to the table, his mother and Félix weren't there.

"Where've they gone?" said Atlas.

"They just went out to check the gate number. They said they'll be right back."

"Oh." Atlas sat down. The others had ordered on his behalf, and at his place there was a bowl of his favourite Tim Hortons chicken noodle soup and a Canadian maple doughnut. He looked at them but didn't eat.

"Tim didn't come?" said Peter.

"No," said Atlas. "I guess I'll never see him again."

"Probably not," agreed Peter. He chewed his egg sandwich for a minute, then put it down and dug in his pocket. He pulled out a ragged booklet made of scribbler pages cut into quarters and then stapled together. "You can have this."

"What is it?"

"All the stuff Tim told you," said Peter, "when you told me. And other stuff we talked about. I wrote it down—you know, the way I write, with drawings and stuff, but I think you can understand it."

Atlas opened the little booklet. There were scattered words in Peter's poor printing and diagrams with arrows and circles. He was touched that Peter had thought all this was worth writing down, and it made him, more than ever, want to be a good big brother—someone who could guide Peter when he needed it.

"But most of this is stuff *I* said, not Tim," said Atlas.

"Well, it's just whatever we talked about afterwards."

Atlas flipped some more. Had he really said all this? Things that made sense? Maybe he *could* be a good big brother.

He saw a drawing of what was clearly him, but with his hair standing on end and his hands in the air and insects leaping all around. It made him laugh, even as he was cringing. In a barely readable scribble underneath was printed: **It's worse not to have the chance to try to give a present.**

"Tim never said that," said Atlas.

"No," said Peter. "I was just thinking about stuff. I don't think I ever gave Dad a present. I was too little."

Atlas folded over the last page. At the top was written, **Dad**, and the rest of the page was blank. "Why's this page empty?"

"I just didn't know what to put. I can't really remember him much, so I didn't have anything to put." Peter said it evenly, as a simple fact, but Atlas thought it was sad. He didn't know what to say about this, so he said, "Thanks, Peter. Now I won't forget anything important."

"I know," said Peter. "You never do."

Atlas heard Peter's simple confidence in him, like always; but now, rather than being afraid, he thought, *Well, I'll do my best, buddy*, and he gave Peter a friendly little shove and said, "We'd better get down to eating. Last Tim Hortons."

CHAPTER THIRTY-TWO

He took the little booklet out of his wallet. It was pressed flat and thin with age and the pencil lines had faded to almost nothing, but he knew it by heart. He turned the pages carefully. There was the drawing called *Why vs. How?* a drawing of a puzzle which represented the unsolvable mysteries of a family, and then the page titled *Brain Attic*, covered in drawings of hockey, friends, crickets, and many other things—all the things, in fact, which Atlas had wished his brain could solve that winter.

"Atlas!" Peter was standing in the doorway, looking delighted. "I didn't know Tim's was in Spain!"

"Peter!" Atlas jumped up to hug his little brother, nearly exactly the same size as him, now they were both grown. Peter thrust his suitcase at him.

"Sorry, I've really gotta go," and he hurried towards the washroom. Atlas ordered a small black for Peter, and a couple of minutes later, his brother sank into the chair opposite.

"So," said Atlas with a twinkle in his eye, "you didn't see him?"

"'Course not. I've never seen him. And nary a sign today. Tim has been laying low for fifteen years."

They both chuckled.

Peter picked up his mug, and Atlas flipped over to the last, unfinished page of the booklet: **Dad**. He remembered how it had frustrated him at first, thinking how unfair it was that Peter had no memories of their father, nothing with which to fill that page. But after a while, he came to accept it. A blank page was always a page for writing a new story, and as Tim would say, *Why, that's something you can do something about*.

Peter was talking about his incomprehensible studies and his oddball colleagues, and already it was making Atlas laugh. Apparently, the absent-minded mad scientist wasn't a nasty, unfounded trope—at least, not in Peter's lab. Atlas tucked away the booklet and his memories, and he leaned in to listen to his brother.

THANK YOU!

Thank you for reading! I'm delighted to share *Tim* with you. If you enjoyed it, leaving a review would be so much appreciated. It helps other readers discover the book.

ABOUT THE AUTHOR

L. L. Rose is from Canada but is currently living and working wherever in the world she decides to go next, and soaking up a lot of material for future stories. She has one daughter who used to travel the globe with her, but is now grown and busy having her own adventures and life back in Canada.

facebook.com/l.l.rose.author

instagram.com/l.l.rose.prose

ALSO BY L. L. ROSE

Mendacities: *A tale of secrets, lies, love—and a lighthouse* (Quandaries book one).

Possession: *a comedy of wrong belongings* (Quandaries book two).

Printed in Great Britain
by Amazon

59215861R00090